# AN UNNECESSARY ASSASSIN

# AN UNNECESSARY ASSASSIN

A COLLECTION OF CRIME AND MYSTERY
STORIES BY BRITISH AUTHORS

20230702:1536

**One Day, One Focus, Ending Polio**
If you would like to find out more about the work to
eradicate polio, visit the website <u>endpolio.org</u>.
World Polio Day is 24th October.

# CONTENTS

# SURVIVING RELATIONS
## A POEM

### JIM TAYLOR

My Dad's brother, Percy, flew gliders,
silently over patchwork fields, the A1, and
　　Margaret's little town.
By some miracle those flimsy, soundless
　　toys stayed aloft.
Unbelieving, I never took up his frequent
　　offers,
to fly over the fields, although he was a
　　qualified instructor.
When he wasn't gliding, he was an officer
　in the St John Ambulance brigade.
At least if the wind dropped, or a wing fell
　　off, after the crash landing,
he could have patched us up and we would
　　have walked home.
On the ground, his record as a driver
　　wasn't the best.
A Renault Dauphine mysteriously rolled
　　over several times.

He emerged unscathed and would laugh
    when you mentioned it.
He had a spell as a barber, with his own
    shop.
We went on Sunday afternoons, opening
    up for us especially,
put on his nifty, white jacket, all his kit in
    the top pocket,
finished us off with a swish of the overall
    and a dab of Brylcreem.
Quick tempered and no patience with
    interferers,
Percy was defiant. You could see it in his
    eyes.
That's what kept him in the air, defying
    the wind, the clouds.
Percy, a true Percival, had polio as a child,
had an iron leg brace.
He would never run.
It didn't stop him doing what he wanted.
Look him in the eyes, and he would look
    straight back, unwavering.
You don't halt a runaway train by asking it
    to stop.

# THE HABIT OF SILENCE

## ANN CLEEVES

Newcastle in November, Joe Ashworth thought, is probably the greyest city in the world. Then running up the steps from the Westgate Road, he realised that he'd been to this place before. His seven-year-old daughter had had violin lessons at school and he'd brought her here for her grade one exam. They'd both been intimidated by the grandeur of the building and the girl's hand had shaken during the scales. Listening at the heavy door of the practice room he'd heard the wobble.

Today there was rain and a gusty wind outside and the sign *Lit and Phil Library open to the public* had blown flat onto the pavement. Taped to the inside door, a small handwritten note said that the library would be closed until further notice. Mixed messages. The exams had taken place on the ground floor, but Joe climbed the stone staircase and felt the same sense of exclusion as when he'd waited below, clutching his daughter's small violin case, making some feeble joke in the hope that she'd relax. Places like this weren't meant for a lad from Ashington, whose family had worked down the pit. When there *were* still pits.

At the turn of the stairs, there was an oil painting on the wall. Some worthy Victorian with a stern face and white whiskers. Around the corner a notice board promoting future events: book launches, lectures, poetry readings. And on the landing, looking down at him, a tall man dressed in black, black jeans and a black denim shirt. He wore a day's stubble but he still managed to look sophisticated.

'You must be the detective,' the man said. 'They sent me to look out for you. And to turn away members and other visitors. My name's Charles. I found the body.'

It was a southern voice, mellow and musical. Joe Ashworth took an instant dislike to the man, who lounged over the dark wood banister as if he owned the place.

'Work here, do you?'

It was a simple question but the man seemed to ponder it. 'I'm not a member of staff,' he said. 'But yes, I work here. Every day, actually.'

'You're a volunteer?' Joe was in no mood for games.

'Oh no.' The man gave a lazy smile. 'I'm a poet. Sebastian Charles.' He paused as if he expected Ashworth to recognize the name. Ashworth continued up the stairs so he stood on the landing too. But still the man was so tall that he had to crick his neck to look up at him.

'And I'm Detective Sergeant Ashworth,' he said. 'Please don't leave the building, Mr Charles. I'll need to talk to you later.' He moved on into the library. The poet turned away from him and stared out of a long window into the street. Already the lamps had been switched on and their gleam reflected on the wet pavements.

Joe's first impression, walking through the security barrier, was of space. There was a high ceiling and within that a glass dome. Around the room a balcony. And everywhere books, from floor to ceiling, with little step-ladders to reach the higher shelves. He stared. He hadn't realised that such a place could exist just over the room where small children scratched out tunes for long-suffering examiners. A young library assistant with pink hair sat behind a counter. Her eyes were as pink as her hair and she snuffled into a paper handkerchief.

'Can I help you?'

The girl hadn't moved her lips and the words came from a small office, through an open door. Inside sat a middle-aged woman half hidden by a pile of files on her desk. She looked fraught and tense. He supposed she'd become a librarian because she'd wanted a quiet life. Now she'd been landed with a body, the chaos of the crime scene investigation and her ordered life had been disrupted. He introduced himself again and went into the office.

'I suppose,' she said. 'You want to go downstairs to look at poor Gilbert.'

'Not yet.' As his boss Vera Stanhope always said, the corpse wasn't going anywhere. 'I understand you've locked the door?'

'To the Silence Room? Oh yes.' She gave a smile that made her seem younger and more attractive. 'I suppose we all watch CSI these days. We know what we should do.'

She gestured him to sit in a chair nearby. On her desk, behind the files, stood a photo of two young girls,

5

presumably her daughters. There was no indication of a husband.

'Perhaps you should tell me exactly what happened this morning.' Joe took his seat.

The librarian was about to speak when there were heavy footsteps outside and a wheezing sound that could have been an out of breath hippo. Vera Stanhope appeared in the doorway, blocking out the light. She carried a canvas shopping bag over one shoulder.

'Starting without me, Joe Ashworth?' She seemed not to expect an answer and gave the librarian a little wave. 'Are you alright, Cath?'

Joe thought Vera's capacity to surprise him was without limit. This place made him feel ignorant. All those books by writers he didn't know, pictures by artists whose names meant nothing to him. What could Vera Stanhope understand of culture and poetry? She lived in a mucky house in the hills, had few friends and he couldn't ever remember seeing her read a book. Yet here she was greeting the librarian by her first name, wandering down to the other end of the library to pour herself coffee from a flask set there for readers' use, then moving three books from the only other chair in the office so she could sit down.

Vera grinned at him. 'I'm a member of the Lit and Phil, pet. The Literary and Philosophical Society Library. Have been for years. My father brought me here to lectures when I was kid and I liked the place. And the fact that you don't get fined for overdue books. Don't get here as often as I'd like though.' She wafted the coffee mug under his nose. 'Sorry, I should have offered you some.' She turned back to Cath. 'I saw Sebastian outside. You said on the phone that he found the body.'

The librarian nodded. 'He's taken to working in the Silence Room every afternoon. We're delighted of course. It's good publicity for us. I'm sure we've attracted members since he won the TS Eliot.'

Vera nudged Joe in the ribs. 'The Eliot's a prize for poetry, sergeant. In case you've never heard of it.'

Joe didn't reply. It wasn't just the smell of old books that was getting up his nose.

Cath frowned. 'You know how Sebastian hates the press,' she said. 'I do hope he won't make a scene.'

'Who else was around?' Joe was determined to move the investigation on. He wanted to be out of this place and into the grey Newcastle afternoon as soon as possible.

'Zoë Wells, the library assistant. You'll have seen her as you came in. And Alec Cole, one of the trustees. Other people were in and out of the building, but just five of us were around all morning.' The librarian paused. 'And now, I suppose, there are only four.'

The Silence Room was reached by more stone steps at the back of the library. This time they were narrow and dark. The servant's exit, Joe thought. It felt like descending into a basement. There was no natural light in the corridor below. The three of them paused and waited for Cath to unlock the heavy door. Inside, the walls were lined by more books. These were old and big, reference texts. Still no windows. Small tables for working had been set between the shelves. The victim sat with his back to them, slumped forward over one of the tables. There was a wound on his head, blood and matted hair.

'Murder weapon?' Vera directed her question to both

of them. Then: 'I've been in this room dozens of times, but this is the first time I've ever spoken here. It seems almost sacrilegious. Weird, isn't it, the habit of silence.' She turned to Joe. 'That's the rule. We never speak in here.'

'I wondered if he could have been hit with the book.' Cath nodded towards a huge tome lying on the floor. 'Could that kill someone?'

Vera gave a barking laugh. 'Don't see why not, with enough force behind it. Appropriate, eh? Gilbert Wood killed with words.'

'You knew him?' Why am I not surprised? Joe thought.

'Oh, our Gilbert was quite famous in his own field. Academic, historian, broadcaster, writer. He's been knocking around this place since I was a bairn and he's turned out a few words in his time.' She turned to Cath. 'What was he working on now?'

'He was researching the library's archives. The Lit and Phil began its life as a museum as well as a library and there's fascinating material on the artefacts that were kept here. Some very weird and wonderful stuff. We thought it might make a book. Another boost to our funds.'

Outside there were quick footsteps and a man in his sixties appeared in the doorway. He was small and neat with highly polished black shoes, a grey suit and a dark tie. Joe thought he looked like an undertaker.

'I was working upstairs,' he said. 'The accounts for the AGM next week. Zoë had to tell me that the police had arrived.' There was a touch of reproach in the voice. He was accustomed to being consulted.

'Please meet Alec Cole.' Cath's words were polite enough but Joe thought she didn't like him. 'He's our honorary treasurer. It's Alec who makes sure we live within our means.'

'A difficult task,' Cole said, 'for any charitable organisation during these benighted times.'

'You knew the deceased?' Joe had expected Vera to take charge of the conversation, but she was still staring at Wood's body, apparently lost in thought.

'Of course I knew him. He was a fellow trustee. We were working together on the restructuring plan'.

Now Vera seemed to wake up. 'What did you make of Gilbert? Got on alright, did you?'

'Of course we got on. He was a charming man. He had plans to make the library more attractive to the public. His research into the archives had thrown up a variety of ideas to bring in a new audience.'

'What sort of ideas?'

'He wanted to develop a history group for young people. History was his passion and he was eager to share it, especially since he retired from the university. He thought we could run field trips to archaeological sites, invite guest lecturers.'

'Aye,' Vera said. 'He tried something like that once before. I remember an outing to Hadrian's Wall. My father thought it would be good for me. It was bloody freezing.'

'It's not so easy to set up field trips these days,' Cath said. 'There are implications. Health and safety. Risk assessment. I wasn't sure it was worth it. Or that we could justify the cost.'

Joe sensed that this was an argument that had played out many times before. He was surprised at Vera allowing the conversation to continue. Today, it seemed, she had no sense of urgency.

'Perhaps we should go upstairs,' he said, 'and talk to the other witnesses.'

'Aye,' the inspector said. 'I suppose we should'. But still her attention was fixed on the dead man. It was as if she were fascinated by what she saw. She bent forward so she could see Wood's face without approaching any closer. Then Ashworth led them away, a small solemn procession, back to the body of the library.

They sat around a large table with the vacuum jug of coffee and a plate of digestive biscuits in the middle. There were six of them now. Sebastian Charles had been called in from the landing and Zoë had emerged from the counter. Joe Ashworth thought she looked hardly more than a child, her face bare of make-up. He saw now that she was tiny, her bones frail as a bird's. The pink hair looked as if she was in fancy dress.

'This is where the old ones sit,' Vera said. 'The retired men and the batty old ladies, chewing the fat and putting the world to rights. Well, I suppose that's what we're doing too. Putting the world to rights. There's something unnatural about having a murderer on the loose.' She looked at them all. 'Who was the last person to see him alive?'

'I saw him at lunchtime,' Zoë said. 'He went out to buy a sandwich, and for a walk, to clear his head, he said. Just for half an hour.'

'What time was that?'

'Between midday and twelve thirty.' Zoë wiped her eyes again. She made no noise, but the tears continued to run down her face. Like a tap with a dodgy washer, Joe thought, only leaking silently. No irritating drips. 'He brought me a piece of cheesecake from the bakery. A gift. He knew it was my favourite.'

'Any advance on twelve thirty?'

Joe found it hard to understand his boss's attitude. She'd known the victim yet there was this strange flippancy, as if the investigation were a sort of game, or a ritual that had to be followed. Perhaps it was this place, all these books. It was easy to think of the murder as just another story.

'We had a brief discussion on the back stairs,' Alec Cole said. 'Just after Gilbert had gone out for lunch, I suppose. He was on his way down to the Silence Room to continue his work on the archives. I'd just gone to the gents. I asked how things were going. He said he'd made a fascinating discovery that would prove the link between one of the early curators of the Lit and Phil Museum and the archaeology of Hadrian's Wall. Esoteric to the rest of us, I suppose, but fascinating to him.'

'Did you notice if anyone else was working in the room?' Vera asked.

'I couldn't see. The door was shut and I was on my way upstairs when Gilbert went in.'

'And if there *were* anyone inside he wouldn't greet Gilbert,' Vera said. 'Because of the rule of silence. So you wouldn't hear anything either way.' She paused. 'What about you, Cath? Did you see him?'

'Just first thing when he arrived. He must have passed the office when he went out to lunch and I always have my door open but I didn't notice him. I'm snowed under at the moment and I only left my desk to go to the ladies or to pour myself a coffee.'

'And then you found him, Sebastian.'

The poet gave a slow, cat-like smile. 'I went down to start work and there he was, just as you saw him. It was a shock, of course, and rather horrible even though I've felt like killing him a few times.'

'You don't seem very shocked!' At last Zoë's tears stopped and now she was angry. 'I don't know how you can sit there and make a joke of it.'

'Not a very good joke, sweetie. And you all know I couldn't stand the man. It would be stupid to pretend otherwise just for the inspector.'

'Why didn't you like him?' For the first time Vera seemed mildly interested.

'He was creepy,' Sebastian said. 'And self-serving. All this work with the archives was about making a name for himself, not raising funds for the library.'

They sat for a moment in silence. They heard the insect buzzing of the central heating system in the background. Joe waited for Vera to comment but again she seemed preoccupied. 'Is the only access to the Silence Room through here?' he asked. Again he felt the need to move things on. The library was very warm and he found the dark wood and the high shelves oppressive. It was as if they were imprisoned by all the words.

'Yes,' Cath said. 'The doors downstairs are locked from our side when the music exams are taking place.'

'So the murderer must be one of you,' Vera said.

She looked slowly round the table. Joe thought again that it was as if she were playing a parlour game, though there was nothing playful in her expression. Usually at the beginning of an investigation she was full of energy and imagination. Now she only seemed sad. It occurred to Joe that the victim could have been just ten years older than her. Perhaps she'd had a teenage crush on him when he'd led her on the field trip to the Roman wall. Perhaps the earlier flippancy had been her way of hiding her grief. Vera continued to speak.

'You'd better tell me now what happened. As I said before, it's unnatural having a murderer on the loose. Let's set the world to rights, eh?'

Nobody spoke.

'Then I'll tell you a story of my own,' she said. 'I'll make my own confession.' She leaned forward so her elbows were on the table. 'I was about twelve,' she said. 'An awkward age and I was an awkward child. Not as big as I am now, but lumpy and clumsy with large feet and a talent for speaking out of turn. My mother died when I was very small and I was brought up by my father, Hector. His passion was collecting: birds' eggs, raptors. Illegal, of course, but he always thought he was above the law. Had a fit when I applied to the police...' Her voice trailed away and she flashed a smile at them. 'But that was much later and perhaps Gilbert had something to do with that too. Gilbert was kind to me. The first adult to take me seriously. He was a PhD student at the university. A geek, I suppose we'd call him now. Passionate about his history. Alec was quite right about that. He listened to me and asked my opinion, more comfortable with a bright kid than with other grown-ups maybe. He bought me little presents.' She looked at Zoë. 'Some things don't change it seems.'

Vera shifted in her seat. Joe saw that they were all engrossed with her story and that they were all waiting for her to continue.

'These days we'd call it grooming,' she said. 'Then we

were more innocent. Hector saw nothing wrong with entrusting me to the care of a virtual stranger for days at a time while we scrambled around bits of Roman wall. He couldn't believe, I suppose that anyone could find me sexually attractive. And to be fair, he assumed that other kids would be there too. At first I revelled in it. The attention. Gilbert had a car and sitting beside him I felt like a princess. He brought a picnic. Cider. My first taste of alcohol. And the arm around my shoulder, the hand on my knee, what harm could there be in that?'

She came to a stop again.

'He sexually assaulted me.' Her voice was suddenly bright and brittle. 'One afternoon in May. Full sunshine and birds singing fit to bust. Skylarks and curlew. We'd climbed onto the moors beyond the wall, to get a proper view of the scale of it, he said. There was nobody about for miles. He spread out a blanket and pulled me down with him. There was a smell of warm grass and sheep shit. I fought back, but he was stronger than me. In the end there was nothing I could do but let him get on with it. Afterwards he cried.' She looked up at them. 'I didn't cry. I wasn't going to give him the satisfaction.'

For a moment Joe was tempted to reach out and touch her hand, but that of course would have been impossible.

'I never told anyone,' Vera said. 'Who would I tell? Hector? A teacher? How could I? I refused to go out with Gilbert again and Hector called me moody and ungrateful. But I should have told. I should have gone to the police. Because the man had committed a crime and the law is all we have to hold things together.'

Vera stood up.

'I don't believe he's changed,' she said. 'He wasn't

stopped, you see. He got away with it. My responsibility. We'll find images of children on his computer, no doubt about that.' She turned to Sebastian Charles. 'You were right. He was a creepy man.'

She paused for a moment. 'So who killed him?' Her voice became gentle, at least as gentle as a hippo's could be. 'You look like a twelve year old, Zoë. Did he try it on with you?'

'No!' The woman was horrified.

'Of course not. It wasn't a child's body he wanted as much as a child's mind. The need to control and to teach.'

Vera turned again, this time to the middle-aged librarian, who was sitting next to her. 'Why don't you tell us what happened?'

Cath was very upright in her chair. She stared ahead of her. For a moment Ashworth thought she would refuse to speak. But the words came at last, carefully chosen and telling.

'He befriended Evie, my elder daughter. When my husband left last year she was the person most affected by our separation. She's always been a shy child and she became uncommunicative and withdrawn. Gilbert had been part of our lives since I first took over here. I invited him to family parties and to Sunday lunch. I suppose I felt sorry for him. And I thought it would be good for Evie to have some male influence once Nicholas left. He made history come alive for her with his stories of Roman soldiers and the wild border reivers. On the last day of the October half term he took her out. Like your father, I assumed other children would be present. That was certainly the impression he gave. Like your father, it never occurred to me that she could come to harm with him.'

'He assaulted her,' Vera said.

'She won't tell me exactly what happened. He threatened her, I think. Made her promise to keep secrets. But something happened that afternoon. It's as if she's frozen, a shell of the child she once was. The innocence sucked out of her. I should be grateful, I suppose, that she's alive and that he brought her home to me.' Cath looked at Vera. 'The only thing she did say was that he cried.'

'So you killed him?'

'I went to the Silence Room to talk to him. I knew he was alone there. Zoë was busy on the phone and didn't notice that I left the office. I asked him what he'd done to Evie. He put his finger to his lips. "I think you of all people should respect the tradition of the Silence Room", he said in a pompous whisper, barely loud enough for me to hear. I shouted then: "What did you do to my child?"' Telling the story Cath raised her voice so she was shouting again.

She caught her breath for a moment and then she continued: 'Gilbert set down his pen. "Nothing that she didn't want me to do," he said. "And nothing that you'll be able to prove." He was still whispering. Then he started work again. That was when I picked up the book he was reading. That was when I killed him. I left the Silence Room, collected a mug of coffee at the top of the stairs and returned to my office.'

Nobody spoke.

'Oh pet,' Vera said. 'Why didn't you come to me?'

'What would you have done, Vera? Dragged Evie through the courts, forced her to give evidence, to be examined? Don't you think she's been through enough?'

'And now?' Vera cried. 'What will happen to her now?'

Joe sat as still as the rest of them but thoughts were

spinning round his mind. What would he have done? *I wouldn't have let my daughter out with a pervert in the first place. I'll never leave my wife.* But he knew that however hard he tried he could never protect his children from all the dangers of the world. And that he'd probably have killed the bastard, too. He stood up.

'Catherine Richardson, I'm arresting you for the murder of Gilbert Wood.' It was Vera, pre-empting him. Taking responsibility. Putting the world to rights.

\* \* \*

*Copyright © 2023 Ann Cleeves*

\* \* \*

Ann Cleeves is the author of over thirty-five critically acclaimed novels, and winner of the CWA Diamond Dagger 2017. She's the creator of detectives Vera Stanhope, Jimmy Perez and Matthew Venn, who can be found in ITV's Vera, BBC1's Shetland and ITV's The Long Call. She lives in Northumberland where the Vera books are set.

Find out more at Anncleeves.com.

# THE BUZZ OF VOLATILITY

## ROB PARKER

It was only after the silence had gone past the point of excruciating, that Christopher excused himself from the table and announced he was going to the bathroom.

That wasn't, however, where he was going.

As he walked down the bare floorboards of the hall, he ignored the bathroom door on the right, and turned left instead, to the back door. As quietly as possible, he left the stifling atmosphere of the house, and gently closed the door behind him. The muted click of the latch was the only announcement of his arrival outside, and into the evening air.

Christopher noticed then that he still had ketchup on his fingers. It was burger night, a family tradition that had long since stopped carrying any weight of enjoyment or affection. He wiped his hands on the front of his jeans, breathed out hard, and looked onto the forest. Opposite the back step were trees as far as he could see, with no boundary line separating the boy from the vast sea of trunks.

*Runaway*.

Run away was all he wanted to do.

The dynamics of the house, and the interplay between himself and his parents, had become so choking, so stifling, so *much*, that he'd thought about running into those trees so often. He thought about running until his lungs hurt, and his legs couldn't make another yard. About drifting into a new phase of life, free from the uncertainty, misunderstandings and unnecessary pressures.

All of that was preferable to staying here for more of *this*.

The evening sun was dipping, and it cast the forest floor beyond in a patchwork of orange spindles, dancing softly to the tune of a breeze he couldn't yet feel – and rather than stay and wait for the inevitable trouble he would be in, he decided to take his destiny in his own hands.

And sprint.

He jumped off the bottom step and suddenly his arms and legs were pumping over the fallen pine needles, trees and shadows and that life left in his wake. Soon the house and the people in it were no longer in sight, and the memory of it faded just for a blissful moment. He didn't want to think about any of that anymore. He was heading forward, to a new future.

Christopher soon found that he could run further and farther that he'd previously imagined. And through the trunks ahead he began to see the whizzing colours of traffic, and the signs of the town's life. Cars crawled by the tree line, blissfully ignorant of the boy with the ketchup-stained pants. He emerged from the pine boughs into a ditch by the road. The traffic was thick, the evening crawl home for so many underway. He wondered what homes they were going to. What love they would find when they got there. What lives they were leading, and where it would take them next.

He decided to walk alongside the road and, in his own way, join the traffic of those heading to whatever was coming next.

But of course, for Christopher, that was uncertain.

He now had to assume that he was a runaway, and that people would eventually come looking for him. That was what happened when 12-year-old boys left their houses without telling their parents where they were going.

But *them*, those people, they wouldn't have listened anyway.

His future now belonged to him and him alone, abruptly immediate as it was. It scared him somewhat to think of how far over the line he had crossed. Some things couldn't be undone. The hurt he'd caused in the last hour would be lasting.

The boy reached an intersection, and considered which way of the three options he should take.

What would grown-ups do?

A grown-up man, like he was now, might go to a bar, because it seemed that in times of uncertainty, a drink of some kind was in order. This was guesswork of course, based on what he'd seen of the men he'd grown up under and around. He'd seen a bar down the right-hand turn off the intersection, its neon lights promising something that he knew would never amount to more than sticky floors, the smell of stale sweat and the buzz of volatility. But those were things, particularly the latter, that grown-ups seemed to preoccupy themselves with, so that's what he himself would pursue too.

Christopher waited at the crosswalk as a couple of the cars blared their horns at him as they fizzed by. He wasn't sure how long he'd been away from the house – surely the alarm of his whereabouts hadn't been raised yet? What were they beeping at? Was this just a regular thing adults did, to hoot and holler at each other in aimless determination with the loudest tools at their disposal? He ignored them and strode on.

The bar appeared just a short walk down the road. By now, the sun had almost gone, and as he approached the front door, the orange of the evening had just about given way to indigo, with a low frosting of pink neon from a sign that read 'Shane's' in a curly script.

As he strode up to glass doors, he somehow felt no anxiety, despite his tender age. But a hand reached across his chest as he made for the threshold, a tall man in a red cap standing over him, a lit cigarette in hand. He was old, weathered, drawn by adult vices such as tobacco and booze, and he regarded Christopher with something like fascination.

'Awful late for a young lad to be out,' the man said, his voice, a razored gargle, but non-threatening.

'Just coming to let my hair down,' replied Christopher, imagining that's how adults talked. The man looked him up and down with wide pupils that were set alongside crows feet so deep they could hold water, a small river system all joining in the corner of the eye. He looked interested, as if Christopher was a specimen he'd heard about but never seen before. A rare fish in a rock pool that held only crabs.

'Why this particular place?' asked the man.

'Why not?'

'Fair enough.'

The man blew smoke into the air, careful not to direct it at the boy, sending it spiralling and contorting over their heads. He wore jeans so torn at the knees they were held together only by a handful of splitting threads, and a green military jacket that had seen more action than any soldier Christopher could imagine. 'Problem is, while I'd love to welcome you inside, it's not the done thing for young lads to be hanging around in bars, now,' the man said.

That didn't settle right with Christopher. He had fallen at the first hurdle.

No, he counselled himself. Not fallen. Just stumbled. A knock from which you could only strengthen and succeed.

He'd had enough of listening to adults – adults who didn't get it, adults who didn't care, adults who didn't understand.

'It's not like you can stop me,' said Christopher taking a step forward – but the man put his hand across the doorway, again careful not to make any physical contact with Christopher himself. 'Actually, it's a lot like I can stop you, considering it's my bar and all.' With the hand he had used to block Christopher's passage, he raised and extended a finger upwards to the neon sign. 'Shane,' he said, then diverted that reaching finger to his own chest.

'What is it with you adults, always finding the need to tell me what to do?' Christopher said.

Shane smiled with the sensitivity of a parent, which

filled Christopher with such distaste he could have retched - then from nowhere, in Shane, it seemed like a penny dropped of some kind. His eyes broadened, his jaw sagged just slightly, and he looked up the street, at the traffic and the cars, then behind him back down in the other direction.

'Actually kid, you know, maybe you should come inside. Maybe you should come in and get off the street, know what I mean?'

Christopher didn't like the sudden change in direction. It betrayed a duplicity, a slipperiness that he'd seen all too often in those adults who were supposed to be looking after him. He took a step back.

'I've seen you kid, that's all, I'm saying,' said Shane, taking a step towards the boy, now with his hands up, palms out. It was then that Christopher knew that the alarm had been raised. He was a boy gone missing. 'You're the kid on TV, the one they're looking for. If you come inside, I'll get you something to drink, and keep you safe until they come and get you. This isn't the kind of place for a kid to be wandering round ... unattended, you understand?'

Christopher took two steps back quickly, saddened in the knowledge that even now, so soon after his break-away, he was being pulled back and inhibited by adults who didn't know the first thing about him — the first thing about anything to do with him. He turned around, shouting over his shoulder: 'You're all the same!'

Christopher didn't even wait to see if Shane went after him, and ran back in the direction he'd come from. He ran back to the intersection, and the crosswalk, where he could see the trees on the other side. Before he really knew what he was doing, he'd automatically started navigating his way home. Like a homing protocol he didn't even know had been installed, he was heading back to that place on autopilot.

He cursed himself.

It was true, and his little foray into the real world had shown him.

He was still just a kid.

Just a kid who couldn't make the big decisions.

That the world wouldn't trust just yet.

As he entered the trees, the darkness swallowed him, the moon a white disk occasionally breaking through the overhanging boughs.

He wondered to himself, why he'd done what he did. And then he thought that he really didn't know.

He just felt so misunderstood, all the time. Those people, his parents, they felt his needs didn't matter and were problematic, despite them being the wants and desires of a child. As he travelled through the trees, he didn't run this time — moreover, he trudged through the pine straw, wary of each knot in the roots on his route. He began to feel a little bit sheepish, but still proud. Like he'd shown them, in a way, what he was really capable of. How strong he really was.

After a while, the back porch light of his home appeared, a distant beacon interrupted by tree trunks. He exited the woods with a fraction of the speed he'd entered them, and as he climbed the back step and put his hand on the back door handle, he tried to work out how long he'd been away.

It could have been as little as half an hour.

It could be as much as a few hours.

He didn't really know.

What he did know, however, was that it was time to face the music. He was a kid in an adult world and that, while true for now, wouldn't last forever. He'd try again one day, and next time would get it right. He opened the back door, and walked back down the darkened hallway into the kitchen. His parents were still around the table. Unmoved and silent. It was like he never left.

"I'm sorry about this,' he said, as he retook his seat. "But when I said I didn't want lettuce, I really fucking meant it.'

He looked at his mum and then at his dad. His mum's throat was still slit, blood all over the table and plates and had even drenched the burger that still sat obscenely in front of her. His dad still had the knife in the side of his neck, buried to the hilt just under his ear, his eyes now filmed over but still stuck in surprise.

'Christopher,' said a voice from behind him. 'You need to get on the floor, with your hands behind your back. Please, young man. Do it slowly.'

Christopher wasn't even angry. He was surprised, that was all.

He turned to look, and a flashlight beam blinded his eyes – but not before he saw the uniform, and the gun. 'On the ground now Christopher, nice and easy.'

He stood slowly, thinking about grabbing the knife from his dad's neck and making another go of it. The flesh had parted easily. He'd love another go at it.

'Don't even think about it, Christopher,' the cop said. So Christopher didn't.

He lowered to his knees, glancing down at the floor – and caught sight of his pants.

It all really did look like ketchup, he thought – as the light rushed forward, he was pushed onto his face and the shouting really started.

\* \* \*

\* \* \*

Rob Parker is a married father of three, who lives in Warrington, UK. The author of the Ben Bracken thrillers, *Crook's Hollow* and the Audible bestseller *Far From The Tree*, he enjoys a rural life, writing horrible things between school runs. Rob writes full-time, attends various author events across the UK, and boxes regularly for charity.

He spends a lot of time in schools across the North, encouraging literacy, story-telling and creative writing, and somehow squeezes in time to co-host the For Your Reconsideration film podcast and appear regularly on The Blood Brothers Crime Podcast. He is also a member of the Northern Crime Syndicate.

# REVENGE IS BEST SERVED COLD

## ZOË SHARP

Layla's curse, as she saw it, was that she had an utterly fabulous body attached to an instantly forgettable face. It wasn't that she was ugly. Ugliness in itself stuck in the mind. It was simply that, from the neck upwards, she was plain. A bland plainness that encouraged male and female eyes alike to slide on past without pausing. Most failed to recall her easily at a second meeting.

From the neck down, though, that was a different story and had been right from when she'd begun to blossom in eighth grade. Things had started burgeoning over the winter, when nobody noticed the unexpected explosion of curves. But when summer came, with its bathing suits and skinny tops and tight skirts, Layla suddenly became the most whispered-about girl in her class.

A pack of the kind of boys her mother was usually too drunk to warn her about took to following her when she walked home from school. At first, Layla was flattered.

But one simmering afternoon, under the banyan and the Spanish moss, she learned a brutal lesson about the kind of attention her new body attracted.

And when her mother's latest boyfriend started looking at her with those same hot lustful eyes, Layla cut and run. One way or another, she'd been running ever since.

At least the work came easy. Depending on how much she covered up, she could get anything from selling lingerie or perfume in a high-class department store to exotic dancing. She soon learned to slip on different personae the same way she slipped on a low-cut top or a demure blouse.

Tonight she was wearing a tailored white dress shirt with frills down the front and a dinky little clip-on bow tie. Classy joint. The last time she'd worn a bow-tie to wait tables, she'd worn no top at all.

The fat guy in charge of the wait staff was called Steve and had hands to match his roving eye. That he'd seen beyond Layla's homely face was mainly because he rarely looked his female employees above the neck. Layla had noted the way his eyes glazed and his mouth went slack and the sweat beaded at his receding hairline, and she wondered if this was another gig she was going to have to try out for on her back.

She didn't, in the end, but only because Steve thought of himself as sophisticated, she realised. The proposition would no doubt come after. Still, Steve only let his pants rule his head so far. Enough to let Layla — and the rest of the girls — know that he'd be taking half their tips tonight. Anyone who tried to hold anything back would be out on her ass.

Layla didn't care about the tips. That wasn't why she was here, anyhow.

Now, she stood meekly with the others while Steve walked the line, checking everybody over.

"Got to look sharp out there tonight, girls," he said. "Mr Dyer, he's a big man around here. Can't afford to let him down."

He seemed to have a thing for the name badges each girl wore pinned above her left breast. Hated it if they were crooked, and liked to straighten them out personally and take his time getting it just so. The girl next to Layla, whose name was Tammy, rolled her eyes while Steve pawed at her. Layla rolled her eyes right back.

Steve paused in front of her, frowning. "Where's your badge, honey? This one here says your name is Cindy and I *know* that ain't right." And he made sure to nudge the offending item with clammy fingers.

Layla shrugged, surprised he picked up on the deliberate swap. Her face might not stick in the mind, but she couldn't take the chance that her name might ring a bell.

"Oh, I guess it musta' gotten lost," she said, all breathless and innocent. "I figured seeing as Cindy called in sick and ain't here—and none of the fancy folk out there is gonna remember my name anyhow—it don't matter."

Steve continued to frown and finger the badge for a moment, then met Layla's brazen stare and realised he'd lingered too long, even for him. With a shifty little sideways glance, he let go and stepped back. "No, it don't matter," he muttered, moving on. Alongside her, Tammy rolled her eyes again.

Layla had the contents of her canapé tray hurriedly explained to her by one of the harassed chefs and then ducked out of the service door, along the short drab corridor, and into the main ballroom.

The glitter and the glamour set her heart racing, as it always did. For a few years, she'd dreamed of moving in these circles without a white cloth over her arm and an open bottle in her hand. And, for a time, she'd almost believed that it might be so.

Not anymore.

Not since Bobby.

She reached the first cluster of dinner jackets and long dresses that probably cost more than she made in a year —just for the fabric, never mind the stitching—and waited to catch their attention. It took a while.

"Sir? Ma'am? Would you care for a canapé? Those darlin' little round ones are smoked salmon and caviar, and the square ones are Kobe beef and ginger."

She smiled, but their eyes were on the food, or they didn't think it was worth it to smile back. Just stuffed their mouths and continued braying to each other like the stuck-up donkeys they were.

Layla had done this kind of gig many times before. She knew the right pace and frequency to circulate, how often to approach the same guests before attentive turned to irritating, how to slip through the crowd without getting jostled. How to keep her mouth shut and her ears open. Steve might hint that she had to put out to get signed on again, but Layla knew she was good and he was lucky to have her.

*Well, after tonight, Stevie-boy, you might just change your mind about that.*

She smiled and offered the caviar and the beef,

reciting the same words over and over like someone kept pulling a string at the back of her neck. She didn't need to think about it, so she thought about Bobby instead.

Bobby had been the bouncer in a roadhouse near Tallahassee. A huge guy with a lot of old scar tissue across his knuckles and around his eyes. Tale was he'd been a boxer, had a shot until he'd taken one punch too many in the ring. Then everything had gone into slow motion for Bobby and never speeded up again.

He wore a permanent scowl, like he'd rip your head off and spit down your neck as soon as look at you, but Layla quickly realised that was merely puzzlement. Bobby was slightly overmatched by the pace of life and couldn't quite work out why. Still plenty fast enough to throw out drunks in a cheap joint, though. And once Bobby had laid his fists on you, you didn't rush to get up again.

One night in the parking lot, Layla was jumped by a couple of guys who'd fallen foul of the 'no touching' rule earlier in the evening and caught the rough side of Bobby's iron-hard hands. They waited, tanking up on cheap whiskey, until closing time. Waited for the lights to go out and the girls to straggle, yawning, from the back door. They grabbed Layla before she had a chance to scream, and were touching all they wanted when Bobby waded in out of nowhere. Layla had never been happier to hear the crack of skulls.

She'd been angry more than shocked and frightened — angry enough to stamp them a few times with those lethal heels once they were on the ground. Angry enough to take their overflowing billfolds, too. But it didn't last. When Bobby got her back to her rented double-wide, she shook and cried as she clung to him and begged him to help her forget. That night she discovered that Bobby was big and slow in other ways, too. And sometimes that was a real good thing.

For a while, at least.

"Ma'am? Would you care for a canapé? Smoked salmon and caviar on that side, and this right here's Kobe beef. No, thank *you*, ma'am."

Layla worked the room in a pattern she'd laid out inside her head, weaving through the crowd with the nearest thing a person could get to invisibility. It was a big fancy do, that was for sure. Some charity she'd never heard of and would never benefit from. The crowd was circulating like hot dense air through a fan, edging their way up towards the host and hostess at the far end.

The Dyers were old money and gracious with it, but firmly distant towards the staff. They knew their place and made sure the little people, like Layla, were aware of theirs. Layla didn't mind. She was used to being a nobody.

Mr Dyer was indeed a big man, as Steve had said. A mover and shaker. He didn't need to mingle, he could just stand there, like royalty, with a glass in one hand and the other around the waist of his tall, elegant wife, looking relaxed and casual.

Well, maybe not so relaxed. Every now and again Layla noticed Dyer throw a little sideways look at their guest of honour and frown, as though he still wasn't quite sure what the guy was doing there.

Guy called Venable. Another big guy. Another mover and shaker. The difference was that Venable had clawed his way up out of the gutter and had never forgotten it. He stood close to the Dyers in his perfectly tailored tux with a kind of secret smile on his face, like he knew they didn't want him there but also knew they couldn't afford to get rid of him. But, just in case anyone thought about trying, he'd surrounded himself with four bodyguards.

Layla eyed them surreptitiously, with some concern. They were huge — bigger than Bobby, even when he'd been still standing — each wearing a bulky suit and one of those little curly wires leading up from their collar to their ear, like they were guarding the president himself. But Venable was no statesman, Layla knew for a fact.

She hadn't expected him to be invited to the Dyers' annual charity ball and had worked hard to get herself on the staff list when she'd found out he was. A lot of planning had gone into this, one way or another.

By contrast, the Dyers had no protection. Well, unless you counted that bossy secretary of Mrs Dyer's. Mrs Dyer was society through and through. The type who wouldn't get out of bed in the morning without a social secretary to remind her. The type whose only job is looking good and saying the right thing and being seen in the right places. There must be some kind of college for women like that.

Mrs Dyer had made a big show of inspecting the arrangements, though. She'd walked through the kitchen earlier that day, nodding serenely, just so her husband could toast her publicly tonight for her part in overseeing the organisation of the event, and she could look all modest about it and it not quite be a lie.

She'd had the secretary with her then, a slim woman with cool eyes who'd frozen Steve off the first time he'd tried laying a proprietary hand on her shoulder. Layla and the rest of the girls hid their smiles behind bland faces when she'd done that. Even so, Steve took it out on Tammy — had her on her back in the storeroom almost before they were out the door.

The secretary was here tonight, Layla saw. Fussing around her employer, but it was Mr Dyer whose shoulder she stayed close to. Too close, Layla decided, for their relationship to be merely professional. An affair perhaps? She wouldn't put it past any man to lose his sense and his pants when it came to an attractive woman. Still, she didn't think the secretary looked the type. Maybe he liked 'em cool. Maybe she was hoping he'd leave his wife.

At the moment, the secretary's eyes were on their guest. Venable had been free with his hosts' champagne all evening and his appetites were not concerned only with the food. Layla watched the way his body language grew predatory when he was introduced to the gauche teenage daughter of one of the guests, and she stepped in with her tray, ignoring the ominous looming of the bodyguards.

"Sir, can I interest you in a canapé? Smoked salmon and caviar or Kobe beef and ginger?"

Venable's greed got the better of him and he let go of the girl's hand, which he'd been grasping far too long. She snatched it back, red-faced, and fled. The secretary gave Layla a knowing, grateful smile.

Layla moved away quickly afterward, a frown on her face, cursing inwardly and knowing he was watching her. She was here for a purpose. One that was too important to allow stupid mistakes like that to risk bringing her unwanted attention. And after she'd tried so hard to blend in.

To calm herself, to negate those shivers of doubt, she thought of Bobby again. They'd moved in together, found a little apartment. Not much, but the first place Layla had lived in years that didn't need the wheels taken off before you could call it home.

He'd been always gentle with Layla, but then one night he'd hit a guy who was hassling the girls too hard, hurt him real bad, and the management had to let Bobby go. Word got out and he couldn't get another job. Layla had walked out, too, but she went through a dry spell as far as work was concerned, and now there were two of them to feed and care for.

Eventually, she was forced to go lower than she'd had to go before, taking her clothes off to bad music in a cheap dive that didn't even bother to have a guy like Bobby to protect the girls. As long as the customers put their money down before they left, the management didn't care.

Layla soon discovered that some of the girls took to supplementing their income by inviting the occasional guy out into the alley at the back of the club. When the landlord came by twice in the same week threatening to evict her and Bobby, she'd swallowed her pride. By the end of that first night, that wasn't all she'd had to swallow.

Even Bobby, slow though he might be, soon realised what she was doing. How could he not question where the extra money was coming from when he'd been in the business long enough to know how much the girls made in tips — and what they had to do to earn them? At first, when she'd explained it to him, Layla thought he was cool with it. Until the next night when she was out in the alley between sets, her back hard up against the rough stucco wall with some guy from out of town huffing sweat and beer into her unremarkable face.

One minute she was standing with her eyes tight shut, wondering how much longer the guy was going to last, and the next he was yanked away and she heard that dreadful crack of skulls.

Bobby hadn't meant to kill him, she was sure of that. He just didn't know his own strength, was all. Then it was his turn to panic and tremble, but Layla stayed ice cool. They wrapped the body in plastic and put it into the trunk of a borrowed car before driving it down to the Everglades. Bobby carried it out to a pool where the 'gators gathered and left it there for them to hide. Layla even went back a week later, just to check, but there was nothing left to find.

They stripped the guy before they dumped him, and struck lucky. He had a decent watch and a bulging wallet. It was a month before Layla had to put out against the stucco in the alley again.

How were they supposed to know he was connected to Venable? That the watch Bobby had pawned would lead Venable's bone-breakers straight to them?

A month after the killing, Venable's boys picked Bobby and Layla up from the bar and drove them out to some place by the docks. Bobby swore that Layla wasn't in on it, that they should leave her alone, let her go. Swore blind that it was so. And eventually, they blinded him, just to make sure.

Layla thought she'd never get the sound of Bobby's screaming out of her head as they'd tortured him into a confession of sorts. But even when they'd snapped his spine, left him broken and bleeding on that filthy concrete floor, Bobby had not said a word against Layla. And she, to her eternal shame, had been too terrified to confess her part in it all, as though that would make a mockery of everything he'd gone through.

So, they'd left her. She was a waitress, a dancer, a hooker. A no-account nobody. Not worth the effort of a beating. Not worth the cost of a bullet.

Helpless as a baby, damaged beyond repair, Bobby went into some institution just north of Tampa. Layla took the bus up to see him every week for the first couple of months. But, gradually, getting on that bus got harder to do. It broke her heart to see him like that, to force the cheerful note into her voice.

Eventually, the bus left the terminal one morning and Layla wasn't on it.

She'd cried for days. When she'd gotten word that Bobby had snuck a knife out of the dining hall, waited until it was quiet then slit his wrists under the blankets and bled out softly into his mattress during the night, there had been no more tears left to fall.

Layla's heart hardened to a shell. She'd let Bobby down while he was alive, but she could seek justice for him after he was dead. She heard things. That was one of the beauties of being invisible. People talked while she served them drinks, like she wasn't there. Once Layla had longed to be noticeable, to be accepted. Now she made it her business simply to listen.

Of course, she knew she couldn't go after Venable alone, so Layla had found another bruiser with no qualms about burying the bodies. And, once he'd had a taste of that spectacular body, he was hers.

Thad was younger than Bobby, sharper, neater, and when it came to killing he had the strike and the morals of a rattlesnake. Layla knew he'd do anything for her, right up until the time she tried to move on, and then he was likely to do anything *to* her instead.

Well, after tonight, she wouldn't care.

She slipped out of the ballroom. Instead of turning into the kitchen, this time she took the extra few strides to the French windows at the end of the corridor. She furtively opened them a crack, then closed them again carefully so they didn't latch.

By the time Layla returned to the ballroom, the canapés were not all she was holding. She'd detoured via the little cloakroom the girls had been given to change and store their bags. What she'd collected from hers she was holding flat in her right hand, hidden by the tray. A Beretta 9mm, hot most likely. As long as it worked, Layla didn't care.

A few moments later someone stopped by her elbow and leaned close to examine the contents of the tray.

"Well hello, *Cindy*." A man's voice, a smile curving the sound of it. "And just what you got there, little lady?"

Thad, looking pretty nifty in the tux she'd made him rent. He bent over her tray while she explained the contents, making a big play over choosing between the caviar or the beef. And underneath, his other hand touched hers, and she slipped the Beretta into it.

"Well, thank you, sugar," he said, taking a canapé with a flourish and slipping the gun inside his jacket with his other hand, like a magician. When the hand came out again, it was holding a snowy handkerchief, which he used to wipe his fingers and dab his mouth.

Layla had made him practice the move until it seemed so natural. Shame this was a one-time show. He would have made such a partner, someone she might just have been able to live her dreams with. If only he hadn't had that cruel streak. If only he'd touched her heart the way Bobby had.

Poor crippled blinded Bobby. Poor *dead* Bobby...

Ah well. Too late for regrets. Too late for much of anything, now.

Layla caught Thad's eye as she made another round and he nodded, almost imperceptibly. She nodded back, the slightest inclination of her head, and turned away. As she did so she bumped deliberately into the arm of a man who'd been recounting some fishing tale and spread his hands broadly to lie about the size of his catch. He caught Layla's tray and sent it flipping upwards. Layla caught it with the fast reflexes that came from years of waiting crowded tables amid careless diners. She managed to stop the contents crashing to the floor, but most of it ended up down the front of her blouse instead.

"Oh, I am *so* sorry, sir," she said immediately, clutching the tray to her chest to prevent further spillage.

"No problem," the man said, annoyed at having his story interrupted and oblivious to the fact it had been entirely his fault. He checked his own clothing. "No harm done."

Layla managed to raise a smile and hurried out. Steve caught her halfway.

"What happened, honey?" he demanded. "Not like you to be so clumsy."

Layla shrugged as best she could, still trying not to shed debris.

"Sorry, boss," she said. "I've got a spare blouse in my bag. I'll go change."

"OK, sweetheart, but make it snappy." He let her move away a few strides, then called after her, "And if that's caviar you're wearing, it'll come out of your pay, y'hear?"

Layla threw him a chastised glance over her shoulder that didn't go deep enough to change her eyes, and hurried back to the little cloakroom.

She scraped the gunge off the front of her chest into the nearest trash, took off the blouse and threw that away, too, then rummaged through her bag for a clean one. This one was calculatedly lower cut and more revealing, but she didn't think Steve would object too hard, even if he caught her wearing it.

She pulled out another skirt, too, even though there was nothing wrong with her old one. This was shorter than the last, showing several inches of long smooth thigh below the hem and, without undue vanity, she knew it would drag male eyes downwards, even as her newly exposed cleavage would drag them up again. With any luck, they'd go cross-eyed trying to look both places at once.

She swapped her false name badge over and took the cheap Makarov 9mm and a roll of duct tape out of her bag. She lifted one remarkable leg up onto the wooden bench and ran the duct tape around the top of her thigh, twice, to hold the nine in position, just out of sight. The pistol grip pointed downwards and she knew from hours in front of the mirror that she could yank the gun loose in a second.

She'd bought both pistols from a crooked military surplus dealer down near Miramar. Thad insisted on coming with her for the Beretta, had made a big thing about checking the gun over like he knew what he was doing, sighting along the barrel with one eye closed.

Layla had gone back later for the Makarov. She didn't have enough money for the two, but she'd been dressed to thrill and she and the dealer had come to an arrangement that hadn't cost Layla anything at all. Only pride, and she'd been way overdrawn on that account for years.

Now, Layla checked in the cracked mirror that the gun didn't show beneath her skirt. Her face was even blander in its pallor and, just for once, she wished she'd been born pretty. Not beautiful, just pretty enough to have been cherished.

The way she'd cherished Bobby. The way he'd cherished her.

She left the locker room and collected a fresh tray from the kitchen. The chefs were under pressure, the activity frantic, but when she walked in on those long dancer's legs there was a moment of silence that was almost reverent.

"You changed your clothes," one of the chefs said, mesmerised.

She smiled at him, saw the fog lift a little as the disappointment of her face cut through the haze of lust created by her body.

"I spilled," she said, collecting a fresh tray. She felt every eye on her as she walked out, smiled when she heard the collective sigh as the door swung closed behind her.

It was a short-lived smile.

Back in the ballroom, it was all she could do not to go marching straight up to Venable, but she knew she had to play it cool. The four bodyguards were too experienced not to spot her sudden surge of guilt and anger. They'd pick her out of the crowd the way a shark cuts out a weakling seal pup. And she couldn't afford that. Not yet.

Instead, she forced herself to think bland thoughts as she circled the room toward him. Saw out of the corner of her eye Thad casually moving up on the other side. The relief flooded her, sending her limbs almost lax with it. For a second, she'd been afraid he wouldn't go through with it. That he'd realise what her real idea was, and back out at the last moment.

For the moment, though, Thad must think it was all going to plan. She stepped up to the Dyers, offered them something from her tray. The secretary still hadn't left his side, she saw. The girl must be desperate.

Layla took another step, sideways toward Venable, ducking around the cordon of bodyguards. Offered him something from her tray. And this time, as he leaned forward, so did she, pressing her arms together to accentuate what nature had so generously given her.

She watched Venable's eyes go glassy, saw the way the eyes of the nearest two bodyguards bulged the same way. There was another just behind her, she knew, and she bent a little further from the waist, knowing she was giving him a prime view of her ass and the back of her newly-exposed thighs. She could almost feel that hot little gaze slavering up the backs of her knees.

*Come on, Thad...*

He came pushing through the crowd nearest to Venable, moving too fast. If he'd been slower, he might have made it. As it was, he was the only guy for twenty feet in any direction who didn't have his eyes full of

Layla's divine body. Venable's eyes snapped round at the last moment, jerky, panicking as he realised the rapidly approaching threat. He flailed, sending Layla's tray crashing to the ground, showering canapés.

The bodyguards were slower off the mark. Thad already had the gun out before two of them grabbed him. Not so much grabbed as piled in on top of him, driving him off his legs and down, using fists and feet to keep him there.

Thad was no easy meat, though. He kept in shape and had come up from the streets, where unfair fights were part of the game. Even on the floor, he lashed out, aiming for knees and shins, hitting more than he was missing. A third bodyguard joined in to keep him down, a leather sap appearing like magic in his hand.

There was that familiar crack of skulls. *Just like Bobby*...

Layla winced, but she couldn't let that distract her now. Her mind strangely cool and calm, Layla stepped in, ignored. The fourth bodyguard had stayed at his post, but Layla was shielded from his view by his own principal, and everyone's attention was on the fight. Carefully, she reached under her skirt and yanked the Makarov free, unaware of the brief burn as the tape ripped from her thigh.

The safety was already off, the hammer back. The army surplus guy down in Miramar had thrown in a little instruction as well. Gave him more of a chance to stand up real close behind her as he demonstrated how to hold the unfamiliar gun, how to aim and fire.

She brought the nine up the way he'd shown her, both hands clasped around the pistol grip, starting to take up the pressure on the trigger, she bent her knees and

45

crouched a little, so the recoil wouldn't send the barrel rising, just in case she had to take a second shot. But, this close, she knew she wouldn't need one, even if she got the chance.

One thing Layla hadn't been prepared for was the noise. The report was monstrously loud in the high-ceilinged ballroom. And though she thought she'd been prepared, she staggered back and to the side. And the pain. The pain was a gigantic fist around her heart, squeezing until she couldn't breathe.

She looked up, vision starting to shimmer, and saw Venable was still standing, shocked but apparently unharmed. How had she missed? The bodyguard had come out of his lethargy to throw himself on top of his employer, but there was still an open window. There was still time...

Layla tried to lift the gun but her arms were leaden. Something hit her, hard, in the centre of her voluptuous chest, but she didn't see what it was, or who threw it. She frowned, took a step back and her legs folded, and suddenly she was staring up at the chandeliers on the ceiling and she had to hold on to the polished wooden dance floor beneath her hands to stay there. Her vision was starting to blacken at the edges, like burning paper, the sound blurring down.

The last thing she saw was the slim woman she'd taken for a secretary, leaning over her with a wisp of smoke rising from the muzzle of the 9mm she was holding.

Then the bright lights, and the glitter, all faded to black.

\* \* \*

The woman Layla had mistaken for a secretary placed two fingers against the pulse point in the waitress's throat and felt nothing. She knew better than to touch the body more than she had to now, even to close the dead woman's eyes.

*Cindy*, the name tag read, under the trickle of the blood. She doubted that would match the woman's driver's licence.

She rose, sliding the SIG semiautomatic back into the concealed-carry rig on her belt. Two of Venable's meaty goons wrestled the woman's accomplice, bellowing, out of the room. She turned to her employer.

"I don't think you were the target, Mr Dyer, but I couldn't take the chance," she said calmly. She jerked her head towards the bodyguards. "If this lot had been halfway capable, I wouldn't have had to get involved. As it was…"

Dyer nodded. He still had his arms wrapped round his wife, who was sobbing, and his eyes were sad and tired.

"Thank you," he said quietly.

The woman shrugged. "It's my job," she said.

"Who the hell are you?" It was Venable himself who spoke, elbowing his way out from the protective shield that his remaining bodyguards had belatedly thrown around him.

"This is Charlie Fox," Dyer answered for her, the faintest smile in his voice. "She's *my* personal protection. A little more subtle than your own choice. She's good, isn't she?"

Venable stared at him blankly, then at the dead

woman, lying crumpled on the polished planks. At the unfired gun that had fallen from her hand.

"You saved my life," he murmured, his face pale.

Charlie stared back at him. "Yes," she said, sounding almost regretful. "Whether it was worth saving is quite another point. What had you done to her that she was prepared to kill you for it?"

Venable seemed not to hear. He couldn't take his eyes off Layla's body. Something about her was familiar, but he just couldn't remember her face.

"I don't know—nothing," he said, cleared his throat of its hoarseness and tried again. "She's a nobody. Just a waitress." He took another look, just to be sure. "Just a woman."

"Oh, I don't know," Dyer said, and his eyes were on Charlie Fox. "From where I'm standing she's a hell of a woman, wouldn't you say?"

\* \* \*

*Copyright © 2023 Zoë Sharp*

\* \* \*

Zoë Sharp spent most of her formative years living aboard a catamaran on the northwest coast of England. She opted out of mainstream education at the age of twelve, and wrote her first novel at fifteen. She began her highly acclaimed series featuring no-nonsense ex-Special Forces trainee turned bodyguard heroine, Charlie Fox, after receiving death-threats in the course of her work as a photojournalist. Her work has been nominated for numerous awards, been used in a Danish school text book, inspired an original song and music video, and been optioned for TV and film. When not working on her novels or short stories, Zoë can be found improvising weapons out of everyday objects, renovating houses, or international pet-sitting. Find out more at zoesharp.com

\* \* \*

*This short story featuring my long-running series protagonist, Charlie Fox, is unusual as it is not written in first person—in Charlie's voice. Instead, the story is that of a waitress and stripper called Layla, who has reached a rock-bottom turning point in her life and has made a momentous decision.*

*This story came about when Megan Abbott invited me to contribute to the anthology of female noir, A HELL OF A WOMAN, which she was editing. The theme of the anthology was to celebrate the girlfriends, secretaries, sisters and other female characters who normally play sidekicks and walk-ons in noir fiction. This was their chance to shine.*

*While I was thinking about what to write for A HELL OF A WOMAN, I had a trip planned by ferry from Scotland across to Northern Ireland. It was a long drive to the ferry port at Stranraer, and traffic was slow and heavy. In brief, I just failed to make the boat, arriving at the port just as the security gates were closing. I had no choice but to hang around in Stranraer for several hours until the next crossing.*

*This was how I ended up sitting in a little café, drinking coffee and idly watching the waitresses moving mostly ignored between the crowded tables. And that's when the character of Layla first began to form.*

*She's seen life from the seamy underside, found and lost*

*love, been discarded, betrayed and abandoned. But now she has a plan...*

*Served Cold was shortlisted for the Crime Writers' Association Short Story Dagger, and was chosen to appear in THE MAMMOTH BOOK OF BEST BRITISH CRIME, edited by Maxim Jakubowski.*

# SAFE ENOUGH

## LEE CHILD

Wolfe was a city boy. From birth his world had been iron and concrete, first one city block, then two, then four, then eight. Trees had been visible only from the roof of his building, faraway across the East River, as remote as legends. Until he was twenty-eight years old the only mown grass he had ever seen was the outfield at Yankee Stadium. He was oblivious to the chlorine taste of city water, and to him the roar of traffic was the same thing as absolute tranquil silence.

Now he lived in the country.

Anyone else would have called it the suburbs, but there were broad spaces between dwellings, and no way of knowing what your neighbor was cooking other than getting invited to dinner, and there was insect life in the yards, and wild deer, and the possibility of mice in the basement, and drifts of leaves in the fall, and electricity came through wires slung on poles and water came from wells.

To Wolfe, that was the country.

That was the wild frontier.

That was the end of a long and winding road.

The road had started winding twenty-three years earlier in a Bronx public elementary school. Back in those rudimentary days a boy was marked early. Hooligan, wastrel, artisan, genius, the label was slapped firmly in place and it stuck forever. Wolfe had been reasonably well behaved and had managed shop and arithmetic pretty well, so he was stuck in the artisan category and expected to grow up to be a plumber or an electrician or an air conditioning guy. He was expected to find a sponsor in the appropriate local and get admitted to an apprentice-ship and then work for forty-five years. Which is precisely how it turned out for Wolfe. He went the electrician route and was ten years into his allotted forty-five when it happened.

What happened was that the construction boom in the suburbs finally overwhelmed the indigenous supply of father-and-son electrical contractors. That was all they had up there. Small guys, family firms, one-truck opera-tions, mom doing the invoices. Same for the local roofers and plumbers and drywall people. Demand outran supply. But the developers had bucks to make and couldn't tolerate delay. So they swallowed their pride and sent flyers down to the city union halls, and followed them with minivans, pick up at seven in the morning, back in time for dinner. They found it easy to compete on wages. City budgets were stalled.

Wolfe was not the first to sign up, but he wasn't the last. Every morning at seven o'clock he would climb into a Dodge Caravan full of stuff belonging to some suburban foreman's kids. A bunch of other city guys would climb in behind him. They would stay silent and morose through the one-hour trip, but they watched out the windows with a degree of curiosity. Some of them were turned out early in a manicured town full of quarter-acre lots. Some of them stayed in until the trees thickened up and they hit the north of the county.

Wolfe was put to work on the last stop up the line.

Anyone who had seen a little more geography than Wolfe would have pegged the place correctly as mildly undulating terrain covered with hundred-year-old second-growth forestation and a few glacial boulders, with some minor streams and some small ponds. Wolfe thought it was the Rocky Mountains. To him, it was unbelievably dramatic. Birds sang and chipmunks darted and there was gray lichen on the rocks and tangled riots of vines everywhere.

His work site was a stick-built wooden house going up on a nine-acre lot. Every conceivable thing was different from the city. There was raw mud under his feet. Power came in on a cable as thick as his wrist that was spliced off another looping between two tarred poles on the shoulder of the road. The new feed was terminated at a meter and a breaker box screwed to a ply board that was set upright in the earth like a gravestone. It was a 200-amp supply. It ran underground in a graveled trench the length of the future driveway, which was about as long as the Grand Concourse. Then it came out in the future basement, through a patched wound in the concrete foundation.

Then it was Wolfe's to deal with.

He worked alone most of the time. Drywall crews were scarce. Nobody was slated to show up until he was finished. Then they would blitz the sheetrock job and move on. So Wolfe was a small cog in a big dispersed machine. He was happy enough about that. It was easy work. And pleasant. He liked the smell of the raw lumber. He liked the ease of drilling wooden studs with an augur instead of fighting through brick or concrete with a hammer. He liked the way he could stand up most of the time, instead of crawling. He liked the fresh cleanliness of the site. Better than poking around in piles of old rat shit.

He grew to like the area, too.

Every day he brought a bag lunch from a deli at home. At first he ate in what was going to be the garage, sitting on a plank. Then he took to venturing out and sitting on a rock. Then he found a better rock, near a stream. Then he found a place across the stream with two rocks, one like a table and the other like a chair.

Then he found a woman.

She was walking through the woods, fast. Vines whipped at her legs. He saw her, but she didn't see him. She was preoccupied. Angry, or upset. She looked like a spirit of the countryside. A goddess of the forest. She was tall, she was straight, she had untamed straw-blonde hair, she wore no make-up. She had what magazines call bone structure. She had blue eyes and pale delicate hands.

Later, from the foreman, Wolfe learned that the lot he was working on had been her land. She had sold nine of thirty acres for development. Wolfe also learned that her marriage was in trouble. Local scuttlebutt said that her husband was an asshole. He was a Wall Street guy who commuted on Metro North. Never home, and when he was he gave her a hard time. Story was he had tried to stop her selling the nine acres, but the land was hers.

Story was they fought all the time, in that tight-ass half-concealed way that respectable people use. The husband had been heard to say I'll f-ing kill you to her. She was a little more buttoned-up, but the story was she had said it right back.

Suburban gossip was amazingly extensive. Where Wolfe was from, you didn't need gossip. You heard everything through the walls.

They gave Wolfe time and a half to work Saturdays and slipped him big bills to run phone lines and cable. Being a union man, he shouldn't have done it. But there were going to be modems, and a media room, and five bedroom phone extensions sharing three lines. Plus fax. Plus a DSL option. So he took the money and did the work.

He saw the woman most days.

She didn't see him.

He learned her routine. She had a green Volvo wagon and he would see it pass the bottom of the new driveway when she went to the store. One day he saw it go and downed tools and walked through the woods and stepped over the property line onto her land. Walked where she had walked. The trees were dense, but after about twenty yards he came out on a broad lawn that led up to her house. The first time, he stopped there, right on the edge.

The second time, he went a little further.

By the fifth time, he had been all over her property. He had explored everything. He had taken his shoes off and padded through her kitchen. She didn't lock her door. Nobody did, in the suburbs. It was a badge of distinction. "We never lock our doors," they all said, with a little laugh.

More fool them.

Wolfe finished the furnace line in the new basement and started on the first floor. Every day he took his lunch to the twin rocks. One time-and-a-half Saturday he saw the woman and her husband together. They were on their lawn, fighting. Not physically. Verbally. They were striding up and down the grass in the hot sunlight and Wolfe saw them between tree branches like they were on a stage under a flashing stroboscope. Like disco. Fast sequential poses of anger and hurt. The guy was an asshole, for sure. Completely unreasonable, in Wolfe's estimation. The more he railed, the lovelier the woman looked. Like a martyr in a church window. Wounded, vulnerable, noble.

Then the asshole hit her.

It was a kind of girly roundhouse slap. Try that where Wolfe was from and your opponent would laugh for a minute before beating you to a pulp. But it worked well enough on the woman. The asshole was tall and fleshy and he got enough of his dumb bulk behind the blow to lift her off her feet and dump her on her back on the grass. She sat up, stunned. Disbelieving. There was a livid red mark on her cheek. She started to cry. Not tears of pain. Not even tears of rage. Just tears of sheer heartbroken sadness that whatever great things her life had promised, it had all come down to being dumped on her ass on her own back lawn, with four fingers and a thumb printed backward on her face.

Soon after that it was the Fourth of July weekend and Wolfe stayed at home for four days.

\* \* \*

When the Dodge Caravan brought him back again he saw a bunch of local cop cars coming down the road. From the woman's house, probably. No flashing lights. He glanced at them twice and started work. Second floor, three lighting circuits. Switched outlets and ceiling fixtures. Wall sconces in the bathrooms. But the whine of his augur must have told the woman he was there because she came over to see him. First time she had actually laid eyes on him. As far as he knew. Certainly it was the first time they had talked.

She crunched her way over the driveway grit and leaned in past the plywood sheet that was standing in for the front door and called, "Hello?"

Wolfe heard her over the noise of the drill and clattered down the stairs. She had stepped inside the hallway. The light was behind her. It made a halo of her hair. She was wearing old jeans and a T-shirt. She was a vision of loveliness.

"I'm sorry to bother you," she said.

Her voice was like an angel's caress.

Wolfe said, "No bother."

"My husband has disappeared," she said.

"Disappeared?" Wolfe said.

"He wasn't home over the weekend and he isn't at work today."

Wolfe said nothing.

The woman said, "The police will come to see you. I'm here to apologize for that in advance. That's all, really."

But Wolfe could tell it wasn't.

"Why would the police come to see me?" he asked.

"I think they'll have to. I think that's how they do

things. They'll probably want to know if you saw anything. Or heard any … disturbances."

The way she said disturbances was really a question, real-time, from her to him, not just a future prediction of what the cops might ask. Like, did you hear the disturbances? Did you? Or not?

Wolfe said, "My name is Wolfe. I'm pleased to meet you."

The woman said, "I'm Mary. Mary Lovell."

Lovell. Like love, with two extra letters.

"Did you hear anything, Mr. Wolfe?"

"No," Wolfe said. "I'm just working here. Making a bit of noise myself."

"It's just that the police are being a bit … distant. I know that if a wife disappears, the police always suspect the husband. Until something is proven otherwise. I'm wondering if they're wondering the same kind of thing, but in reverse."

Wolfe said nothing.

"Especially if there have been disturbances," Mary Lovell said.

"I didn't hear anything," Wolfe said.

"Especially if the wife isn't very upset."

"Aren't you upset?"

"I'm a little sad. Sad that I'm happy."

Sure enough the police came by about two hours later. Two of them. Town cops, in uniform. Wolfe guessed the department wasn't big enough to carry detectives. The cops approached him politely and told him a long and rambling story that basically recapped the local gossip. Husband and wife on the outs, always fighting, famous for it. They said upfront and man to man that if the wife had disappeared they'd have some serious questions for the husband. The other way around was unusual but not unknown and, frankly, the town was full of rumors. So, they asked, could Mr. Wolfe shed any light?

No, Mr. Wolfe said, he couldn't.

"Never seen them?" the first cop asked.

"I guess I've seen her," Wolfe said. "In her car, time to time. Leastways, I'm guessing it was her. Right direction."

"Green Volvo?"

"That was it."

"Never seen him?" the second cop asked.

"Never," Wolfe said. "I'm just here working."

"Ever heard anything?"

"Like what?"

"Like fights, or altercations."

"Not a thing."

The first cop said, "This is a guy who apparently walked away from a big career in the city. And guys don't do that. They get lawyers instead."

"What can I tell you?"

"We're just saying."

"Saying what?"

"The load bed on that Volvo is seven feet long, you put the seats down."

"So?"

"It would help us to hear that you didn't happen to look out the window and see that Volvo drive past with something maybe six-three long, maybe wrapped up in a rug or a sheet of plastic."

"I didn't."

"She's known to have uttered threats. Him too. I'm telling you, if she was gone, we'd be looking at him, for sure."

Wolfe said nothing.

The cop said, "Therefore we have to look at her. We have to be sensitive about equality. It's forced on us."

The cop looked at Wolfe one last time, working man to working man, appealing for class solidarity, hoping for a break.

But Wolfe just said, "I'm working here. I don't see things."

Wolfe saw cop cars up and down the road all day long. He didn't go home that night. He let the Dodge Caravan leave without him and went over to Mary Lovell's house.

He said, "I came by to see how you're doing."

She said, "They think I killed him."

She led him inside to the kitchen he had visited before.

She said, "They have witnesses who heard me make threats. But they were meaningless. Just things you say in fights."

"Everyone says those things," Wolfe said.

"But it's really his job they're worried about. They say nobody just walks away from a job like his. And they're right. And if somebody did, they'd use a credit card for a plane or a hotel. And he hasn't. So what's he doing? Using cash in a fleabag motel somewhere? Why would he do that? That's what they're harping on."

Wolfe said nothing.

Mary Lovell said, "He's just disappeared. It's impossible to explain."

Wolfe said nothing.

Mary Lovell said, "I would suspect myself too. I really would."

"Is there a gun in the house?" Wolfe asked.

"No," Mary said.

"Kitchen knives all accounted for?"

"Yes."

"So how do they think you did it?"

"They haven't said."

"They've got nothing," Wolfe said.

Then he went quiet.

Mary said, "What?"

Wolfe said, "I saw him hit you."

"When?"

"Before the holidays. I was in the woods, you were on the lawn."

"You watched us?"

"I saw you. There's a difference."

"Did you tell the police?"

"No."

"Why not?"

"I wanted to talk to you first."

"About what?"

"I wanted to ask you a question."

"What question?"

"Did you kill him?"

There was a tiny pause, hardly there at all, and then Mary Lovell said, "No."

It started that night. They felt like conspirators. Mary Lovell was the kind of suburban avant-garde bohemian that didn't let herself dismiss an electrician from the Bronx out of hand. And Wolfe had nothing against upscale women. Nothing at all.

Wolfe never went home again. The first three months were tough. Taking a new lover five days after her husband was last seen alive made things worse for Mary Lovell. Obviously. Much worse. The rumor mill started up full blast and the cops never left her alone. But she got through it. At night, with Wolfe, she was fine. The tiny seed of doubt that she knew had to be in his mind bound her to him. He never mentioned it. He was always unfailingly loyal. It made her feel committed to him, unquestioningly, like a fact of life. Like she was a princess and had been promised to someone at birth. That she liked him just made it better.

* * *

After three months the cops moved on, mentally. The Lovell husband's file gathered dust as an unsolved case. The rumor mill quieted. In a year it was ancient history. Mary and Wolfe got along fine. Life was good. Wolfe set up as a one-man contractor. Worked for the local developers out of a truck that Mary bought for him. She did the invoices.

\* \* \*

It soured before their third Christmas. Finally Mary admitted to herself that beyond the bohemian attraction her electrician from the Bronx was a little ... boring. He didn't know anything. And his family was a pack of wild animals. And the fact that she was bound to him by the tiny seed of doubt that had to be in his mind became a source of resentment, not charm. She felt that far from being clandestine co-conspirators they were now cell-mates in a prison constructed by her long-forgotten husband.

For his part Wolfe was getting progressively more and more irritated by her. She was so damn snooty about everything. So smug, so superior. She didn't like baseball. And she said even if she did, she wouldn't root for the Yankees. They just bought everything. Like she didn't?

He began to sympathize vaguely with the long-forgotten husband. One time he replayed the slap on the lawn in his mind. The long sweep of the guy's arm, the arc of his hand. He imagined the rush of air on his own palm and the sharp sting that would come as contact was made.

Maybe she had deserved it.

One time face to face in the kitchen he found his own arm moving in the same way. He checked it inside a quarter-inch. Mary never noticed. Maybe she was shaping up to hit him. It seemed only a matter of time.

The third Christmas was where it fell apart. Or to be accurate, the aftermath of the third Christmas. The holiday itself was OK. Just. Afterward she was prissy. As usual. In the Bronx you had fun and then you threw the tree on the sidewalk. But she always waited until January sixth and planted the tree in the yard.

"Shame to waste a living thing," she would say.

The trees she made him buy had roots. He had never before seen a Christmas tree with roots. To him, it was all wrong. It spoke of foresight, and concern for the long-term, and some kind of guilt-ridden self-justification. Like you were permitted to have fun only if you did the right thing afterward. It wasn't like that in Wolfe's world. In Wolfe's world, fun was fun. No before, and no after.

Planting a tree to her was cutesy. To him it was a back-breaking hour digging in the freezing cold.

They fought about it, of course. Long, loud, and hard. Within seconds it was all about class and background and culture. Furious insults were thrown. The air grew thick with them. They kept on until they were physically too tired to continue. Wolfe was shaken. She had reached in and touched a nerve. Touched his core: No woman should speak to a man like that. He knew it was an ignoble feeling. He knew it was wrong, out of date, too traditional for words.

But he was what he was.

He looked at her and in that moment he knew he hated her.

He found his gloves and wrapped himself up in his down coat and seized the tree by a branch and hurled it out the back door. Detoured via the garage and seized a shovel. Dragged the tree behind him to a spot at the edge of the lawn, under the shade of a giant maple, where the snow was thin and the damn Christmas tree would be sure to die. He kicked leaf litter and snow out of his way and plunged the shovel into the earth. Hurled clods deep into the woods. Cut maple roots with vicious stabs. After ten minutes sweat was rolling down his back. After fifteen minutes the hole was two feet deep.

After twenty minutes he saw the first bone.

He fell to his knees. Swept dirt away with his hands. The thing was dirty white, long, shaped like the kind of thing you gave a dog in a cartoon show. There were stringy dried ligaments attached to it and rotted cotton cloth surrounding it.

Wolfe stood up. Turned slowly and stared at the house. Walked toward it. Stopped in the kitchen. Opened his mouth.

"Come to apologize?" Mary said.

Wolfe turned away. Picked up the phone.

Dialed 911.

* * *

The locals called the State Troopers. Mary was kept under some kind of unofficial house arrest in the kitchen until the excavation was completed. A State lieutenant showed up with a search warrant. One of his men pulled an old credenza away from the garage wall and found a hammer behind it. A carpentry tool. Dried blood and old hair were still clearly visible on it. It was bagged up and carried out to the yard. The profile of its head exactly matched the hole punched through the skull they had found in the ground.

At that point Mary Lovell was arrested for the murder of her husband.

* * *

Then science took over. Dental, blood and DNA tests proved the remains to be those of the husband. No question about that. It was the husband's blood and hair on the hammer, too. No question about that, either. Mary's fingerprints were on the hammer's handle. Twenty-three points of similarity, more than enough for the locals, the State Police, and the FBI all put together.

Then lawyers took over. The county DA loved the case to bits. To put a middle-class white woman away would prove his impartial even-handedness. Mary got a lawyer, the friend of a friend. He was good, but overmatched. Not by the DA. By the weight of evidence. Mary wanted to plead not guilty, but he persuaded her to say yes to manslaughter. Emotional turmoil, temporary loss of reason, everlasting regret and remorse. So one day in late spring Wolfe sat in the courtroom and watched her go down for a minimum ten years. She looked at him only once during the whole proceeding.

Then Wolfe went back to her house.

He lived there alone for many years. He kept on working and did his own invoices. He grew to really love the solitude and the silence. Sometimes he drove down to the Stadium but when parking hit twenty bucks he figured his Bronx days were over. He bought a big-screen TV. Did his own cable work, of course. Watched the games at home. Sometimes after the last out he would sit in the dark and review the case in his head. Cops, lawyers, dozens of them. They had done a pretty thorough job between them.

But they had missed two vital questions.

One: With her pale delicate hands, how was Mary Lovell accustomed to handling hammers and shovels? Why did the local cops right at the beginning not see angry red blisters all over her palms?

And two: How did Wolfe know exactly where to start digging the hole for that damn Christmas tree? Right after the fight? Aren't cops supposed to hate coincidences? But all in all Wolfe figured he was safe enough.

\* \* \*

*Copyright © 2023 Lee Child*

\* \* \*

After being made redundant from his job because of corporate restructuring, James Grant decided to start writing novels, stating they are "the purest form of entertainment."

In 1997 his first novel, *Killing Floor*, was published, and he moved to the United States in the summer of 1998. He starts each new book of the series on the anniversary of starting the first book after losing his job.

His pen name "Lee" comes from a family joke about a heard mispronunciation of the name of Renault's Le Car, as "Lee Car". Calling anything "Lee" became a family joke. His daughter, Ruth, was "lee child".

Find out more at jackreacher.com.

# SWAN SONG

## CAROLINE ENGLAND

Taking in the sparkling street lights, festive shop windows and the aroma of roasted chestnuts, I stroll through our pretty high street and think of you. It's bustling with cheery figures and faces, and yet it seems muffled too. By the dense downfall of snow, probably, or perhaps it's just me as memories of the glinting canal trickle back.

Derived from an ancient stream that runs through the village, the name Lymm means a 'place of running water', and it was that which attracted us here eight years ago. But today I leave this corner of Cheshire. The move has taken me the best part of two days and now I'm back to hand the keys to the new owner, Mrs Salus, and find Dolos, our cat. To stop him from straying, I kept him inside, shutting him in as each room was emptied, but as I loaded the last of that life in the removal van, I knew I had to let him explore the wildlife, the rustles and redolence of the riverbank one last time. So I rubbed his paws with butter, opened the back door and gave him his freedom.

Now at number seven, I put down the cat basket and take a final tour of the shell which once was our home. The furniture all gone, only the piano stool remains. An echo of the music, a reminder of the past, of you.

Forlorn in its emptiness, only imprints have endured in our front room: the dent of sofa legs in the thinning carpet, a groove in the wall where your cello rested, the cobweb shadows where smiling photographs hung. And fingerprints; so many smudges of love beneath light switches, on handles and door edges; up the staircase wall, tiptoeing to our room at the top where everything had seemed possible.

Remember when I'd pack a picnic and we'd hitch a ride or take the bus from our student accommodation, walk and talk, then find secluded woodland and make heady love at a weekend? Once we'd discovered Spud Wood, Lymm became our favourite destination. We'd amble up the dingle and explore the stunning scenery and sunset around the dam, or take the steep track into Slitten Gorge and follow the streamside path to the site of the ancient slitting mill. Holding hands and stealing kisses, we'd stroll along the towpath of the Bridgewater Canal, peer into the eclectic mix of barges and boats, and speculate about the lives of the people inside.

'How about we purchase one to live in, make love and melodies day in and day out?' you asked one spring morning.

You had such devotion in your eyes, it made my heart

ache. Though we'd both studied music at university and had graduated now, I'd supported your decision to hold out for a 'proper' job as a cellist, and I was happy to work long, dull hours in an office to pay our rent.

'I'm all for that,' I replied lightly. 'But there's just the wee catch of us having no money.'

'I'll make it big one day. Just you see. Then I'll buy you...' He pointed to one of the detached, gated houses I always called my 'dream home'. 'I'll buy you that.'

'Promise?'

'Yup.'

'Faithfully? Or the sarnies are all mine,' I replied, snatching our packed lunch and hurtling along the grassy path to the bridge.

When you caught me up, you circled my waist and made to push me into the water.

'I know you wouldn't. You'd be lost without me!' I laughed. 'You know - cooking, cleaning, looking after your physical, mental and spiritual wellbeing.'

'Well, no one would see me do the dastardly deed at this leafy spot, but...' You held me so tightly, it felt as though your body fused with mine. 'I would be lost. Completely. Adoring you forever is the one thing that I'm sure of.'

\* \* \*

How thrilled we were to be met by a whole army of dashing Santas on our first visit here in December. They were soon followed by a handsome Dickensian carthorse leading a spectacular Christmas parade. Breathing in the crispy air and a wave of sheer emotion, I absorbed the brightly dressed street entertainers, the mellow sounds of the brass band and carol singers, the twinkling fairy lights, festive stalls and lit candles. But it was the rosy-cheeked, smiling children that made me determine to be part of this; I wanted a son or daughter of ours to grow and thrive in this joyful community.

'Let's move here and have babies,' I said.

In my dream world we'd have bought that fabulous detached backing onto the water. The reality was to rent a cheap place on the outskirts of the village, but to my surprise an end of terrace property became available for sale on Lymm Quay. I soon saw from the particulars that the low price and the words 'potential to improve' was a reflection of its dreadful state, but when I climbed to the top room on our viewing and glimpsed a pair of swans blithely cruising the glistening canal, I knew with hard work and dedication, we could make the gutted rooms our forever home.

Though I loved to hear you play your cello, *Le Cygne* was the one piece which brought back my missing musical past. How I loved the gorgeous melody and the imagery of the graceful, long-necked bird calmly gliding over the water, but as time went on, the soulful tempo instilled different feelings of longing and the fleeting nature of happiness.

'The ancient Greeks and Romans believed a swan is mute until its final moments of life, when it sings the most beautiful of all birdsongs,' I once said to you.

'Hmm. From the trumpeting calls, whistles and snorts we hear through the bedroom window, we know that isn't true,' you replied. You kissed the tip of my nose. 'But swans mate for life, and that one's for certain.'

\* \* \*

Two, five and seven years passed without the pregnancy I yearned for. The broodiness always peaked at Christmas time and it got to the point where the envy was so sharp, I couldn't bear to witness the happy families at the village carnival.

'January is around the corner. Can we try for our baby this year?' I asked you.

'We will soon, I promise.' You stroked Dolos's soft fur. 'And for now you have this little chap to love.'

I was fond of the cat, but I wanted a child. 'He seems to prefer the floozy at number nine,' I said, trying for humour. Then, 'You've said "soon" before. We're not getting any younger...'

'I know. But if I'm to be a father, I want to be in a position to properly support us. That will happen, I promise, both the money and our baby. It takes time to build a reputation, but word is spreading and some work is coming in.' You kissed my forehead. 'You've already seen the benefit.'

I still slaved all hours to keep us afloat, and the 'benefit' seemed to relate solely to your drinking too much whisky and buying rounds in the Barn Owl, but I still believed in you.

\* \* \*

The doorbell of our old home brings me back to today. When I open up, Mrs Salus bustles in with a pink nose and several bags. 'Ooh, it's nippy out there, but the joys of Christmas are definitely in the air. I hear there's a procession through the village in a while.'

'There is indeed.' I hand her the keys. 'I hope you'll be happy here.'

'Thanks, love.' She looks uncertain, but grasps my hand. 'By the way, I'm sorry for your loss, especially considering... The neighbour told me. I didn't know whether to say anything but it felt wrong not to.'

'That's kind of you. Thank you.' I puff out the stab of grief. 'I'll search for my cat, then I'll be off.'

My faith in you came good. Word did spread, your talent was recognised and more performances and commissions dribbled in. As spring approached, the blossom, the budding cattails and fluffy goslings prompted me to broach the subject of babies again, but when I arrived home after a tough day in the office, it took agonising moments to work out what I was seeing.

A packed suitcase, your cello and your sheepish face...

'I'm leaving,' you said.

'What? Why would you say that? I thought we were happy,' I replied, that cliché people say when their whole world, their certainty and meaning is whisked away in the beat of two words.

'It isn't that. It's just... Well, I need some space for my music. Creative freedom, I suppose. Just for a while. I'm sorry, it's nothing personal...'

\* \* \*

Over the next months, your lack of contact, the loss and devastation was so unbearable that I couldn't work, couldn't eat, couldn't sleep, and the top room became my prison. But a familiar rap at the door one evening told me you were home. I longed to be bold, to reject your apology, your pleas to come in; I so wanted to shrug and say, 'Nothing personal, but no thanks.'

Yet even as I rushed down the stairs my heart was already soaring with pleasure, relief, alleviation. You'd had your 'space'; you'd missed me; you were back.

'I've come for the piano stool,' you said when I flung open the door. 'It is an antique and I did buy it, so... Look, I'm sorry. There's no one else, I promise, but I have to move on, well, musically. You must understand that.'

The blow took my breath, but I needed to hold onto you just a little bit longer. 'Of course. How about a goodbye drink at the Barn Owl before you go?'

\* \* \*

Lifting my collar, I now trudge the narrow ginnel behind the terraces, calling Dolos's name. Despite the buttered paws, he doesn't appear, so I walk two doors up to number nine and ring the doorbell. Knowing the 'old floozie' is in, I gave it a minute before peering through a crack in her curtains. Far from enjoying his freedom on the banks of the canal, Dolos is stretched out, plump and satisfied, in front of a roaring fire.

\* \* \*

Perhaps if I'd stayed with you for longer in the pub, things might have turned out differently. When the police finally hauled you out of the murky depths of the water, they told me you'd been stumbling your way home to me.

'According to the bartender, he became emotional after you left and said that he'd made a mistake.' The officer smiled thinly. 'But he moved on to doubles, so it was no wonder he was confused and lost his footing on the bridge. Drowning isn't a nice way to go, but the pathologist says it'd have been quick. I hope that's some comfort to you.'

So you were, after all, lost without me.

I leave Dolos's basket outside number nine and nod to myself. Though his perfidy stings, it feels apt he should stay with you by the canal.

'Hello, love? Before you go...' The sound of Mrs Salus's voice pierces my thoughts. 'Your piano stool,' she calls. 'It's a beautiful piece; don't you want to keep it?'

I suppose it's now mine, along with the waterside 'dream home' I bought with the insurance payout. 'No thanks,' I reply. 'You have it or sell it. It's probably worth a bob or two.' I rub my huge, pregnant belly. 'I have this little reminder.'

I inwardly smile. Yes, a reminder of the music you took from me, the promises you made. And your betrayal. *'There's no one else, I promise,'* you said. But your gaze... Oh, how it had flickered. Yet even then a solution had pushed through my haze of anger and despair. There'd been no need to take my contraceptive pills during your absence, but I had maintained the life assurance payments. Of course you could never resist a nightcap or two and, as we'd ambled along the dark towpath towards the Barn Owl, the suggestion of a 'quick cuddle' in Spud Wood for old times' sake.

* * *

Infused with the spirit of Christmas, I hurry to join the parade through the village. As the exquisite cello melody floods my mind, I picture the lone female swan calmly glide over the glassy surface of the water.

And the male? It turned out he *was* mute in his final moments of life.

Just a splash, and then silence.

* * *

* * *

CWA Dagger shortlisted Caroline England is known as the 'Duchess of dark domestic noir'. Her psychological suspense thrillers are *Beneath the Skin*, the top ten e-book bestseller *My Husband's Lies*, *Betray Her*, *Truth Games* and *The Sinner*. *The Stranger Beside Me* will be published on 3rd August 2023.

Caroline also pens gothic-tinged psychological thrillers as CE Rose. Standalone *The House of Hidden*

*Secrets* was followed by *The House on the Water's Edge* and *The Shadows of Rutherford House*. *The Attic at Wilton Place* was published on 30th March 2023.

*Watching Horsepats Feed the Roses* and *Hanged by the Neck* are her dark, twisty short story collections.

# THE FINAL REEL

## AN INSPECTOR MCLEAN SHORT STORY

### JAMES OSWALD

**Monday**

'What've you got for me, Bob?'

Detective Inspector Tony McLean ducked under the police tape and entered the dingy apartment. A dying fly battered itself against a grimy window, and there was a damp smell about the place, old mould and unemptied garbage. Something worse. He followed his nose into the smallest room. It wasn't much wider than the ancient cludgie it held, but three men had managed to squeeze in there. DS Grumpy Bob Laird, a SOC photographer and the deceased.

'I'd say he died a few days ago. Massive trauma to the head,' Bob said. McLean peered closer, wished he hadn't.

'Pulled the chain and the whole cistern came off the wall,' Bob continued. 'It had to weigh a good hundred pounds.'

'A tragic accident then.' McLean stepped back to let Bob out of the room. The photographer's flash popped a couple more times and then he too backed out.

Cleared, McLean could see the whole scene now. The cistern was still attached to the pan by its thick lead pipe. The brackets had come out of the wall and the whole thing had tipped forward, smashed into the victim's head. Death would have been instant.

'RIP Shuggy Brown,' McLean said.

'You know him?'

'Small time cat burglar. Used to go through the death notices in the papers and do over the empty houses.'

'Oh, aye, the Obituary Man. I remember,' Bob said.

McLean looked at the dead figure in front of him, the cistern flopped to one side, its brackets still fixed to it. The bare wooden floorboards were dark with damp, but not soaked.

'Who turned the water off?' He stepped forwards into the room, stared up at the pipe. It had sheared off neatly where it would have entered the cistern.

'No one, as far as I know,' Bob said. 'Neighbours complained of a smell. We forced entry. Called in as soon as we found him.'

'Hmm.' McLean leant over the recumbent corpse, trying hard not to breathe. There were four small holes in the wall above his head, where the cistern had been attached. A century of thick paint had left two bracket-shaped marks. Looking down, he saw the old brass screws lying behind the pan, two to each side. Their heads were also glossed with a thick coat of paint.

'Maybe not an accident then.'

**Tuesday**

*"The actress Shauna Zapata, who died last month at the age of a hundred and two, was cremated today in a private ceremony at Mortonhall Crematorium. Shauna, best known for her Hollywood career in the inter-war period, returned to her home town of Edinburgh in the mid sixties. A recluse, it's understood that she spent her latter years, and the fortunes of her late three husbands, on tracking down all original prints of her roles. Film historians had hoped that she would bequeath this invaluable archive to the nation, but it was revealed today that her entire body of work was cremated with her."*

McLean flicked off the radio and peered through the rain-smeared windscreen at the line of traffic snaking along Clerk Street. Edinburgh was its usual grey, a vicious wind throwing the moisture around the square-cut buildings like a child in a tantrum. Cocooned from it by his metal box, and with the heater working for a change, he was happy just to crawl along. Dan McFeely wasn't going anywhere in a hurry.

The apartment was in Newington, respectable enough without being too ostentatious. A uniform let him in the front door and he climbed four flights of stone stairs worn smooth by countless passing feet. Gloss green walls peeled with damp, stained by a hundred years of salts leaching from the sandstone. On the top landing, a rusty old bicycle frame was padlocked to the railings, its wheels and saddle long gone. Everything smelled faintly of cat piss.

'He's this way, sir. He's in the bath.' Another uniform showed McLean into the apartment. Inside it was a different world, neat and tidy, ordered. Expensive works of art hung on the walls and everywhere there were shelves of pottery figurines, silver figures, collectibles.

The bathroom was small, with a skylight high in the roof. Dan McFeely lay in a pool of scummy red water, one arm dangling over the tub, the other resting on his pale white hairy chest. He head was tilted back as if he were staring at the sky through the little square porthole. A neat gash ran under his pointy chin from one ear to the other.

'He's been here awhile,' the uniform said.

'Let me guess, the neighbours complained about the smell?' McLean could almost taste the tang of iron in the air.

'No sir,' the uniform said. 'I was going house to house, asking about the schoolyard muggings. I knocked and the door swung open.'

'And you came looking for him in the bathroom?'

'That door was open too, sir. I think he might have left them like that on purpose. To be found.'

'What d'you mean?' McLean asked. Then he noticed it, red and shiny in the blood-stained hand. A cut-throat razor.

'Shite.'

'Sir?'

'This is Dan McFeely, sergeant,' McLean said. 'Feely the Fence. See all that stuff out there? That's stolen goods, only he knows we've no way of proving it. The dodgy stuff he's always kept hidden, but he's a cocky bastard who likes to show off how much cleverer he is than us. If he committed suicide, then I'm in line to be the next Pope.'

\* \* \*

'Death would appear to have been caused by heart failure due to acute loss of blood.' McLean stood silently, watching as the pathologist poked and prodded the white body on the slab.

'Loss of blood would appear to be a result of the severing of the carotid artery with a sharp blade. A cut-throat razor such as that found in the subject's left hand. However, appearances would be deceiving in this matter. Whilst a great deal of blood has been lost, there is more still in the body than would be consistent with such a death.'

'What?' McLean asked.

'I'm saying,' the pathologist fixed him with a withering glare. 'That he didn't die from this wound. He was good as dead already when it was inflicted on him. What's more, the cut goes from left to right, and the blade was found in his left hand.'

'What did kill him then?'

'I can't be sure, but he's got some interesting bruising on his neck around the incisions. I'll have to do some tests to be sure, but he could've been strangled first.'

\* \* \*

**Wednesday**

Half past four and it was already dark. Sometimes McLean hated Edinburgh and mostly that was during the winter months. Dark when you got up, dark long before the working day was over. If his working day could ever be said to be over.

The house stood back from the road, screened from the traffic by a high wall and mature trees. It was a substantial building; three storeys of blackened sandstone and tall windows. Grumpy Bob met him at the door and they stepped inside.

'Gabriel Squire,' Bob said.

'The art collector, I know. What's the story?'

'His housekeeper found him.' Bob pointed to a slight woman, sitting on the other side of an entrance hall.

'Mrs Davey, this is Detective Inspector McLean,' Bob said as the housekeeper looked up. Her eyes were red with crying, her cheeks drained of colour. 'Could you tell him what you told me.'

'I was just cleaning the house, like I do every Thursday,' the woman said. 'Mr Squire was in his study. I don't go in there. But I heard voices, you see. Mr Squire shouting at someone. I ... I ... was listening at the door. I know I shouldn't, but Mr Squire, he's ever so nice a gentleman. I couldn't bear it if he was... Well then I heard a woman scream "It's mine, give it to me." And then there was this terrible crash.' Mrs Davey stopped, the tears welling in her eyes.

'Perhaps I'd better have a look,' McLean said to Bob.

A huge fireplace dominated one end of the study and a large desk sat under the window, strewn with odd items. Most of the walls were lined with bookcases and cabinets filled with curios. A body lay sprawled across the hearth.

Gabriel Squire had been in his late fifties, fit, with a full head of greying hair. He wore a velvet smoking jacket, a silk cravat around his neck. Rather incongruously, McLean thought, he sported a pair of fading tartan bathies on his feet. And a large bloody mess where his left temple ought to have been.

'Looks like he tripped over the rug. Hit his head on the

fireplace.' Bob pointed to a skin-and-hair bloodstain on the carved stone.

'What a way to go,' McLean said. 'Killed by an Adam. But what about this woman?'

'Don't know about that sir,' Bob said. 'Mrs Davey... Well, I don't think she's playing the full team, if you know what I mean. She says she knocked, and when she didn't get an answer, she came in. Found him dead. Called us straight away.'

McLean crossed over the room to the window. It was latched, a thick layer of paint gumming it up. He doubted it had been opened in years. There was only the one door. His eyes fell on the desk and its collection of curios; jewellery mostly, small stuff but expensive. McLean was no great expert, but he knew diamonds when he saw them. And craftsmanship. An intricately carved silver figurine instantly put him in mind of Dan McFeely's apartment, and in the midst of it all sat a small round tin, perhaps ten inches across and an inch deep. There was something about it that was almost mesmeric. Perhaps because it looked so out of place. Only years of instinct stopped him from picking it up. Instead, he went back into the hall where Mrs Davey was being comforted by a WPC.

'Has Mr Squire had any unusual visitors recently? Say in the last week?' He asked.

The housekeeper made a strange face, as if thinking about things didn't come naturally to her. She started to shake her head, then stopped.

'There was a gentleman. Last Thursday it would have been. He didn't stay long.'

'Wait here a moment.' McLean went back to his car.

On the back seat the Dan McFeely case file sat amidst a mound of other paperwork and detritus. He fished a picture out of it. Mortuary shot of just the head.

'Was that him?' He asked Mrs Davey. She looked at it nervously.

'Yes, I think so. Only he doesn't look at all well there. He wasn't nearly so pale.'

At the mortuary, McLean gazed down on the naked body and wondered why it was his old friend Angus Cadwallader, the city pathologist, had called him in. Gabriel Squire had been cleaned up, but the ugly wound to his head was still the most obvious sign of his violent end.

'You'd think he died from the blow to the temple,' Cadwallder said. 'But in actual fact he was dead before he hit the fireplace. I understand it was an Adam?'

'Stolen from Auchencruive,' McLean said. 'It turns out that Mr Squire was quite the collector of other people's antiques. So what killed him then, heart attack?'

'No. He was throttled. Quite violently.' The pathologist beckoned McLean over for a better look, what he'd taken for shadows actually mottled skin below the cadaver's chin. 'His windpipe's been crushed and there's severe bruising to his neck. The odd thing is that when we undressed him for the post mortem, his cravat was still perfectly tied.'

\* \* \*

**Thursday**

'This piece is exquisite. Eighteenth century. Made by ourselves, of course.'

McLean sat in a small office at the back of Hamilton and Inches. Across a tiny desk, an elderly man was peering through an eyeglass at one of the silver figurines found at Gabriel Squire's house.

'Do you know who it was sold to?'

'It was part of a set of nine, commissioned by the seventh Marquis of Queensberry. See, it has a number on the base? That was your stick number for the day's shooting. It came back to us in the seventies, part of an auction to raise funds to pay death duties. My predecessor, Mr Mayfield, liked to buy back our more exceptional work whenever he could.'

'So it was stolen from you?' McLean asked.

'Stolen? Heavens no,' the old man said. 'We sold this piece to Mrs McLeod not more than a year ago.'

'Mrs McLeod?'

'You'd probably know her better by her stage name, Shauna Zapata. Such a shame she died. She was one of our best customers. Had a good eye. No, this piece belongs to her estate.'

**Friday**

It took McLean only five minutes to decide he didn't like Kiernan McTavish. The solicitor was executor for the will of the late Shauna McLeod. He was also shifty, never letting his eyes settle anywhere. He fidgeted constantly. And he was evasive.

'Mrs McLeod's worldly goods have all been accounted

for,' he said, barely looking at the small silver figurine. 'They're to be auctioned at Sotheby's at the end of the month. All proceeds will go to the Children's Hospital.'

'So you're sure there was no burglary. Nothing's gone missing. None of these items.' He laid out a number of pictures on the desk. McTavish pounced on them like a clumsy cat. Anything was better than having to look McLean in the eye. He watched as the lawyer peered at each photo, hoping for a spark of recognition. Nothing.

'Or this?' He asked, finally, placing a photograph of the circular tin in front of the lawyer. 'It's a roll of eight mil film. But it's so old and rotten no-one can tell what's on it.'

'Nope,' McTavish said, just a little too quickly. Something like fear flitted across his face and all of a sudden he stopped fidgeting, looked straight at McLean. 'Do you know anything about Mrs McLeod?' he asked.

'Only what I read in the papers. And I've seen a couple of her movies on the telly.'

'Shauna McLeod was a troubled woman,' McTavish said, his voice suddenly formal, as if he were summing up before the jury. 'After her third husband died, she began to believe she was cursed. She thought that every film she'd made had taken a little piece of her soul. So she set about trying to get them back. She tracked down and bought every original printing of every movie she ever appeared in. Every screen test. Every gag reel. Even the cuttings that had found their way into the hands of collectors. She found them all, and she bought them all.'

'And then she had them all cremated alongside her. I heard it on the radio. They had to close Mortonhall down for the day.' McLean said.

'Quite, Inspector,' McTavish said. 'And she was a meticulous woman. Everything was catalogued. Everything. It was stipulated in her will that if her wishes were not carried out, then I... That is to say, we would not receive our fee. It was a not inconsiderable sum, which is why, Inspector, I am perfectly certain that none of these items belonged to Mrs McLeod at the time of her death.'

McLean took back the photographs.

'Well, thank you for your time, Mr McTavish,' he said.

'I'm glad I could be of help. Tell me, Inspector. What happens to those?'

'These? Technically they belong to the estate of Gabriel Squire, but since they were among other items identified as stolen they'll be treated as the same.'

'And?' McTavish was fidgeting again.

'We'll hang onto them for a couple of months and if no-one's claimed them they'll be put up for auction.'

'I see. Well. Thank you Inspector. Goodbye.'

* * *

**A couple of months later**

It was an expensive car; a nineteen-sixties Bristol still as shiny and polished as the day it rolled out of the factory. McLean looked through the windscreen at the body of Kiernan McTavish. His face had turned blue.

'Not something you see much of these days,' said Grumpy Bob. 'It doesn't work with modern cars. You just get a nasty headache.'

'Quite,' McLean looked up at the house and then back to the car. How long was it since he had spoken to McTavish? He knelt down by the open door, reached in and turned the key. It was dead, no juice in the battery. But it was in the 'on' position. He looked at McTavish. The lawyer was relaxed, as if he had fallen asleep, but there was a livid bruise around his neck.

'How'd we find out about him?'

'Neighbour called. Said the car had been left running all night. Uniform came round to have a quiet chat about being more considerate.'

McLean looked around the interior of the car, all leather and polished walnut, shiny chrome and Bakelite switches. A piece of paper was scrumpled into a ball in the footwell by the pedals. He unravelled it. An auction receipt for five hundred pounds, paid for lot 786, plus fifteen percent commission. Cash sale. Dated yesterday.

'Anyone had a look in the house?' McLean asked.

'Not yet, why?'

'Because this man was murdered, then put in here to make it look like suicide. Sound like a familiar MO to you?'

'Gabriel Squire?' Bob asked.

'And Dan McFeely, and I'm thinking Shuggy Brown too. The burglar, the fence, the client and the lawyer. But who? And why? Get a SOC team down here, Bob. I'm going to have a quick nosey inside.'

Outside, the house was classic Edinburgh West End Georgian. Inside it had been stripped down to a white painted minimalist shell. The floors were dark polished wood, the doors the same. The hallway held nothing but a tall metal hatstand. McLean slipped on a pair of latex gloves, then pushed open the nearest door.

It led into the sitting room, which looked out onto the driveway in front through a tall bay window. There were no curtains, just the flimsiest of white canvas blinds, rolled up to the ceiling. A living gas flame fire flickered in a brutal square stone fireplace beneath a wall-mounted plasma television as big as a cinema screen. A white leather sofa faced both. The only other furniture in the room was a desk made from a sheet of glass suspended between two metal trestles. Lying on top of this was lot 786. The tin.

McLean prised the lid off with his thumb, eyes watering at the smell of decomposing celluloid. There wasn't much left of the film, just a vaguely spiral gooey black mess. He touched it lightly with one finger and it slid towards the edge of the tin, revealing a corner of stained paper label underneath. Flipping the tin over delicately, he tried to get the sticky goo to drop into the lid. It oozed out in great strings, then suddenly dropped with a noise like a dying trifle. He held the tin up to the light, peering at the indistinct words on the darkened paper.

Shauna and Morag. Summer 1919. Balnakiel.

'It's mine! Give it to me now!'

McLean tried to whirl around, but all he could feel was hands at his throat. Powerful fingers cut off his breathing in an instant, choked him so that he couldn't even shout for help. Instinctively he dropped the tin and reached up for his attacker. His vision was already narrowing, stars popping in his eyes.

'Mine I tell you! Mine!' A woman's voice, mid-Atlantic accent, familiar. His hands were at his throat now, but he couldn't find her hands, even though he could feel them squeezing the life out of him. Then he saw her, reflected in the glass tabletop.

Long blonde hair tumbling over her shoulders, she looked like some dame from a detective movie. She was dressed for the part, too. Thirties chic, all the rage once again, and she had her hands around his throat. She was choking the life out of him. He'd seen her before. In black and white.

But she wasn't there. She couldn't be there.

McLean reached out blindly for the lid of the tin. The remnants of celluloid lay inside it, oozing out into a sticky black puddle. He could feel his strength fading as his fingers grasped at the edge.

And then he had it. With a last effort, he flung it as hard as he could in the direction of the fireplace.

McLean stared up at the smiling face of Grumpy Bob from his hospital bed. The sergeant had brought a big bag of grapes and was slowly eating his way through the lot of them. 'The SOC boys were well pissed that you torched their crime scene,' he added. 'And the chief wants to know what you were doing in there in the first place. But it could be worse.'

'How so?' McLean asked, then wished he hadn't. His throat hurt even when he thought about swallowing and his face felt like he'd been asleep in the sun for a week. No one had let him near a mirror so he had no idea how much hair he still had.

'Well,' Grumpy Bob said, popping the last grape into

his mouth, scrumpling up the bag and throwing it in the vicinity of the bin. 'You could be dead.'

\* \* \*

\* \* \*

James Oswald is the author of twelve novels in the Edinburgh-based Inspector McLean series. The most recent, *All That Lives*, was published in February 2022. He is also the author of three Constance Fairchild books, No *Time To Cry*, *Nothing To Hide* and the latest, *Nowhere To Run*. As J D Oswald he has written the five-book fantasy epic, *The Ballad of Sir Benfro*, published by Penguin. In his spare time, James runs a 350-acre livestock farm in Fife, where he raises pedigree Highland cattle.

# CAN'T STOP THE SCREAMING

## F.E. BIRCH

*Her screams cut through the morning mist like an animal caught in a snare, the sort of noise that brings tears to your eyes and makes you want to stop and investigate but you don't because you're frightened of the horror you might find so you avoid the noise, turn a different corner and wonder for the rest of your life if you could have done something to make it better.*

\* \* \*

It's early in the morning and she's too far away for the neighbours to hear so her high-pitched screams remain unheard for a little longer. She stands and screams in monotone, black and white, raw and hurting. She knows not what to do so she screams some more. She hardly breathes. Just screams.

It takes six minutes for her mother to find her but to Natalie it could have been an hour, a day, a month, a lifetime. It was her lifetime for she has all but forgotten what life was like before he was there. The day her mother said she had someone for her to meet. She thought it was another little girl, someone for her to play with, to be friends with. But it wasn't. It was him. It was Martin. Natalie stands and screams and remembers a day that most would say she was too young to remember...

* * *

*My safe little home has intruders. Something's going on and the usual quiet day with my mum is broken. Life in our home is gentle, not at all like this. It's just me and mum but this weird day has loud music that plays and plays on. There are people. They disturb me, gathering around me, disrupting my peace.*

*Our cubby hole of a kitchen has worked hard to produce the food above me sitting on the tabletop as I hide beneath, trying to melt behind a wooden leg, hoping not to be seen, wishing to be invisible. The door opposite me stands open but I don't want to go outside. This is my home. I am safe in here. Sun streams in and bounces onto the linoleum in sun-drops. I want to hide in my dark haven under the table like a lump of Sunday carrot fallen from my plate onto the floor, forgotten.*

*A man comes toward me, laughing with his large white teeth. He's big, dark and not funny. He tries to pick me up. I'm too big to be picked up. I'm a big girl, for a little girl.*

*'No!' I want to scream. He steps towards me and I see his black shoes and I smell their polish. They're shiny. I want to reach out, to touch, but I'm scared. I shrink further behind the table leg and clench my eyes tight. I hope the big people will go away. When I open my eyes, I want them to be gone. I flick an eyelash but ladies' legs and men's trousers, the noise and laughter, they tell me they're still here. The big people have smoking sticks, and they make me cough.*

*Mum bends down to me, smiling. She smells of perfume and the smoking sticks, just like the others. Today she wears an orangey-sickly lipstick that I haven't seen before and a blue flowered dress with a little white collar. The dress is short, and she pulls at the hem. She strokes her honey-coloured nylons as she leans towards me. She wants me to come out from under the table, but I won't. I shrink back against the fake wood panelled wall that is all the fashion. I remain fast beneath the table and she hands me a special treat. Chocolate with a rich purple wrapper covering a thin silver foil. It's all mine.*

*It's too much.*

*I can't help it.*

*I start to cry.*

*She peels the paper and gives me the chocolate, leaving me to enjoy this one-off treat of Dairy Milk. I sit, ignored and happy to be so. I want these people to leave, especially the big man with dark hair and polished shoes and the white smoking stick. And his deep dark eyes that look at me in a strange way. The man who said he was to be my father.*

'He's your daddy now,' her mother says, smiling with eyes that twinkle wet. 'And we love him very much, don't we Natalie?'

Natalie looks up at her mother and sees the flowers in her blonde hair that looks lighter, and the pleading on her lips that look pinker. Natalie raises a thumb to her mouth and doesn't blink as she holds her mother eyes.

Her mother sweeps Natalie's thumb away. 'Big girls don't suck thumbs.'

Natalie hears the tut and frustration in her mother's

voice. She also sees the smile break out on her face when she rubs her bulging tummy that stretches the fabric of her wedding dress. Natalie falls against her mother's covered legs, hugs them tight, and in little girl whispers she says, *'Mummy, mummy, mummy.'*

Mummy bends down and hugs Natalie, kissing her round cheek and squeezing her close. The smell of mummy and the sweet smell of the flowers in her hair swims around Natalie's head and for that moment when she closes her eyes, she wants to remember that sweet smell forever. And never wants to forget it.

Martin's voice interrupts, fake-jolly and jealous. 'How's my two special girls then?' He laughs, bends down to join in the hug, but takes it over and Natalie can hardly breathe.

She sees his shiny polished shoes and starts to cry. She knows they think it's a good thing to be a family. Natalie thinks it's not but it's not the sort of thing she can talk about to mummy because she hasn't the words to say what she means, to tell her how she feels. All she knows is that today is the beginning of a different kind of life, the sort of life that belonged to other children, not to her. And she wishes it could all be normal but knows it will never be her sort of normal again.

Natalie is a girl who is different. She knows she's different, not because he said she was, but because the wind blows through her hair and whistles a tune that other girls don't hear, and other girls don't sing. It's the sound of the sea lapping on the early morning shore where one solitary seagull pulls and tugs at a resistant sandworm. It's the lament that rattles around old buildings that have stood the test of time when they should have been demolished but nobody wants to destroy the history. It's the tune of old salt, tangy vinegar, and earthy peas that mingle together to make a northern supper of fish and chips and a carton of mushy peas. She's the girl you can't take the accent from no matter how anyone tries because she keeps it as her own and nobody who cares can listen to it for she doesn't speak.

She's the girl with a memory that she wants to be one of those deus-ex-machina kind of things, one of those endings that Mrs Fletcher, her English teacher, keeps talking about. Mrs Fletcher hates them, deus-ex-machina endings. She says they mustn't be used to finish a story. But Natalie wants the memory to be one of those days with one of those endings.

*It was all a dream.*

'Those endings aren't good endings,' Mrs Fletcher says. 'They lack imagination and leave an unsatisfactory feeling in the head and the heart of the reader like a bad taste on the tongue. Unsavoury. You can do better than that. You can always do better than that.' Natalie knows all about unsavoury things and she doesn't like them either.

'A deus-ex-machina is a writer's lazy way out of a plot,' Mrs Fletcher tells the class. 'With some imagination you can make anything happen with words on the page. You master the story and tell it your own way. Don't take the coward's way out.'

Natalie knows exactly what her teacher means. It's cowardly.

It is like a bad dream that would leave nasty images that flash through her head for the rest of the day once she'd woken up. When she finds her him, her *dad*, at the bottom of the garden hanging from a dirty thick rope, it feels like it should be a dream. She wishes it was a dream. She wants to wake up and shake the dream away like she does when the cold icy snowflakes land on top of her head on a snowy day. She wishes it was a dream, but it is not. That would be the easy way out.

This is Martin's way, the coward's way. It is both the end and the beginning of the nightmare.

Martin. Such a nice name. Such a plain name. An innocuous name. Natalie likes that word. Innocuous. She looks it up on Google to find out what it means. Harmless. Inoffensive. Innocent. Safe. Bland. Yes, he could be bland. But there was nothing innocent or safe or harmless about Martin. The man her mother loved. The man everyone loved. Except for her. Except for Natalie.

Martin is the man her mother married when her sister was in her mother's tummy. Her mother doesn't know she remembers. She thinks Natalie believes he is her father. But Natalie knows he's not. She knows she's the daughter from another man, not Martin, the man her mother married, the man who is father to her two younger sisters. He is not her real father but tells everyone he is.

He tells Natalie she's the girl of his dreams and she sings to him like her mother never has. She knows she doesn't really sing to him, that he uses language as metaphors, those things Mrs Fletcher likes. Natalie doesn't sing because she cannot sing, not anymore. She was singing, but it was a different song, and everyone was deaf to her.

He knew she had changed. He knew that she was close, so close, to opening up the box that once open could never be locked again, and it would make everything change.

He knows and she knows he knows because he had read the story she had written for homework for Mrs Fletcher. Her story was one of metaphor without a deus-ex-machina ending. She hadn't written an ending and she didn't want one of those endings, that *it was all a dream,* but she didn't know how it would end. Not then. Not when she wrote it.

He tells her that it doesn't matter, that she'll be with him forever, for always. There was no hiding place for his beautiful girl, his mermaid, Natalie, who isn't his daughter but is. The girl he taught to swim in a cute kind of doggy-paddle way before she knew how to do the crawl. The girl he took into the water and did those things to when nobody was looking. And everything else he did, knowing she wouldn't tell because she couldn't as she didn't have the voice to speak, to sing, to say, because once he'd come into their lives, she never spoke at all.

A mute. An elective mute. A girl who they said chose not to speak, not because she couldn't, but because she didn't want to. She sang but none of them heard.

He knew Mrs Fletcher would read it and he knew she would understand.

Natalie knows he made sure it was her that found him because he will never leave her, he'll always be in her dreams and her nightmares and her every waking thought. He will always be there. Forever and ever. He made sure of it.

This is no deus-ex-machina. This is real and this is the nightmare.

As his body sways and the snowflakes fall, she shakes her head and keeps on screaming.

\* \* \*

\* \* \*

F.E. Birch is an ex-cop from the North East but she's not a Geordie. She is a prolific short story writer with a trail of pseudonyms and publications behind her. With a penchant for dark, deep and disturbing, her crimes are rarely cosy. She has self-published two collections of competition-winning short stories and her debut novel, *She's Not There* was published in early 2023 by Red Dragon. Harper Collins also published a collection of her stories about life as an undercover cop.

With a bendy EDS body, GSOH and a tad clumsy, she wears many hats and loves wigs. Her friends call her Effie.

# REVENGE IS BEST SERVED HOT

## ROBERT SCRAGG

'You've got a bloody nerve showing your face here.'

The words shoot out like bullets, but Charlie Ford doesn't flinch. He's faced down enough real ones in four decades of running one of London's most notorious crime families.

The man before him screws up his face like he's just sniffed a fart. Seventy if he's a day. Broad Glaswegian, with a face that looks more lived in than a squat.

'It's ok, Pat,' a voice floats across the room.

A young woman walks towards Charlie. Takes him a beat to recognise her from her pictures. Ailsa Baird. Logan's youngest.

Confusion creases across Pat's face, but he doesn't question Ailsa. Even so, the look he gives Charlie could curdle milk. Pat backs away muttering, and Charlie steps forwards to take the hand that Ailsa extends.

'Ailsa Baird, as I live and breathe. Don't think I've seen you since all that terrible stuff with your brother. You must have been, what, four? Five?'

She smiles, but it's all business, no real warmth. Somewhere in her early thirties if he remembers rightly. Flaming red curls cascade across her shoulders like a shawl. Same piercing blue eyes as her dad.

'I've done a lot of growing up since then, Mr Ford.'

'Please,' he says, flashing a toothy grin that would make a Great White proud, 'call me Charlie. I'm so sorry for your loss,' he adds. 'Your dad and I might not always have seen eye to eye, but we always respected each other.'

'If you say so,' she says, turning side on to welcome him inside. The two oversized bodyguards who drove him up to Stirling bookend him as he strides in, stopping to soak in his surroundings. The curtains have been scooped back, flooding the room with pale sunlight. Chandeliers float above his head, dangling from the ceiling like low hanging fruit. An arc of tables encircles the room, largely empty, most mourners preferring to mingle in the centre.

He's only been to the Golden Lion once before. Back when the two families had nearly gone to war. Supposedly neutral territory even though Logan Baird's family had roots here that stretched back centuries before he'd set up shop in Glasgow.

He'd met Logan in this very room. Looked him in the eye and swore on a stack of bibles that he had no idea where his son was. He'd told the truth that day. He hadn't a clue. Still doesn't.

That's what happens when you get asked the wrong questions though. Gives you the chance to skirt around the truth. Tip-toe past it.

'I'll be honest with you, Mr Ford,' Ailsa says, folding her arms. 'There's not many in this room that want you here. But my Dad planned every detail of today from where he'd be, right down to the music and the food. He wanted you here to chat with his successor about what happens next, you know, business-wise.'

Charlie frowns like he's misheard her.

'Where he'd... What? He's ... here? Like actually here?'

Ailsa nods towards the throng of dark suited people spread across the room.

'The funeral is this afternoon. Gives folk the chance to say goodbye in person first.'

Charlie feels the hairs on the back of his neck prick up. 'Like I said,' he says, 'mutual respect. Shame we never got to bury the hatchet properly while he was alive. Least I can do to come up here and see him off though.'

'Interesting choice of words,' Ailsa says. 'See him off. There's still those who think that's what you did to my brother.'

'Now, now Ailsa. That's all ancient history, and like I said back then, I ain't got the foggiest where Dougie went. Broke my Janine's heart, that brother of yours.'

Charlie flashes back thirty years. A regrettable affair. His own daughter Janine, mixed up with Douglas Baird. Charlie still remembers the tornado-like temper descending when he saw Douglas leaving Janine's flat early that morning.

How he'd offered the young Scot a lift, pretences of a protective father wanting to give a lecture. What he dished out that day went far beyond a talking to though. Charlie can still hear how the young lad had begged for his life, face battered and bruised like fruit gone bad. How he pleaded right up until the moment Charlie dropped a breezeblock on him to shut him up once and for all. But he genuinely has no idea where the lad's body is. Had one of his men take care of it.

Rumours of foul play followed Dougie's disappearance, especially when it came out that he'd been seeing Janine on the sly. Regular little Romeo and Juliet playing out right under the family's noses. It had been enough to spark off a three-month long battle between the Bairds and the Fords, before the other families in London and Glasgow stepped in to broker a truce.

Ailsa shrugs it off and says, 'Tell you what, why don't I grab you and your boys a plate, while you pay your respects.'

She's gone before he can answer. The crowd parts like the Red Sea, and he catches a glimpse of a long pine box, brass handles glinting in the light, over by the far wall.

The two lumps of muscle go to follow him as he walks towards it, but he motions for them to sit down. He's Charlie fucking Ford. Bullet-proof. Backed by the coalition of London families. You'd have to be off your rocker to even contemplate giving him so much as a dirty look. Anything happens to him and they'll raze the whole bloody city of Stirling to the ground.

He makes his way through the mourners, until he's two feet from the coffin. Peering down, he sees the peaceful, waxy pallor of his one-time adversary. Logan Baird was a huge man in life. Both in stature and presence. But death has a way of cutting everyone down to size. He's decked out in a pinstripe suit, leather gloves covering his hands.

Charlie studies the face of a man he once wished dead. For a surreal second, he braces himself for the eyes to snap open. Doesn't even realise he's holding his breath until he feels the pressure building in his chest. He forces himself to let it out slow, like air escaping a tyre.

The truce, such as it's been, has been a delicate one. More than once, word has reached his ear about someone sniffing around, looking for word about Dougie Baird. The truth would have been like a match dropped in petrol. At least now, it can die a death.

*A bit like Logan*, Charlie thinks, suppressing a smile.

He heads back to the table, where his bodyguards are tucking into plates piled high with chips and battered sausage. Could be worse. Could be a deep-fried Mars Bar. They'll literally fry anything up here. As he reaches them, Ailsa appears at his elbow, sliding a plate onto the table. The tang of vinegar drifts up, tickling his taste buds, reminding him the last thing he ate was a cold pasty five hours and three hundred miles ago.

'Thank you,' he says, reaching for the first chip before he's even in his seat.

'You're very welcome,' she says, sliding into the seat beside him.

He reaches for the sausage, with batter so crisp he can feel the crunch as his fingers close around it.

'So, you said your Dad wanted his successor to sit down and talk business. Who's the new main man? Want to make sure I catch them before I head home.'

'You already are,' she says.

Charlie stops, mouth open, about to take a bite. He frowns.

'You what?'

'I've been overseeing most of Dad's business for the past five years, Mr Ford. We can talk while you eat.'

'You?' he asks, note of incredulity. 'Taking over the lot?'

'Taken,' she says, very matter of fact. 'Past tense. Dad's been mostly retired for a while. We just didn't advertise it that widely.'

Only takes him a second to regain his composure. He flashes a grin. A wolf eyeing up the sheep. Easy pickings, he thinks.

'Let's talk business then,' he says. 'I was thinking...'

'If you don't mind,' she cuts across him. 'I can probably save you some time.'

'I'm all ears,' he says, spreading his hands, sausage waving in his grip like a conductor's wand.

'As of today, there is no business to talk about. Not with you at least.'

'You've got a lot to learn, girlie,' he says, shaking his head, biting into the sausage. He's just thinking how best to put her in her place when his teeth clamp on something hard enough to jar his jaw. He pulls the sausage out. Holds it up, grimacing in disgust.

'The fuck is this?' he says, stripping away the batter with his free hand.

It's like peeling off a sock. Golden brown gives way to something grey and mottled. He jerks back in his seat, dropping it back onto the mountain of chips.

Charlie glances up to see Ailsa smiling, flash of triumph in her eyes. He shoots out a hand towards her but strong arms pin his back to his sides. He shoots a panicked glance at his men, only to see them both staring straight ahead, hands partially raised thanks to pistol barrels jammed against the base of their necks, held there by two grim faced mourners.

'Big mistake,' he says, locking eyes with Ailsa. 'Huge.'

'The only mistakes here are yours,' she says, voice as calm as a millpond.

'You stupid little girl,' he spits out.

'Is that how you spoke to my brother?'

'I've told you, I...'

'I know, I know. You don't know where he is. I do though.'

It slips in like a sucker punch, stunning him into silence.

'Took me best part of five years, and a shit load of money, but finally heard stories about one of your old heavies. How he bragged about dropping a dozen bodies in a building site one of your rivals used for the same thing, then turned into flats. Had it as insurance against you and them in case anyone tried to put him in concrete boots one day.'

'Bollocks,' he manages, hearing and hating the tremor in his voice. 'Load of bollocks.'

'I bought the building, Charlie. Dug up the basement and brought Dougie home.'

She reaches down, wrapping a napkin around the discarded food, sloughing off the last flakes of batter to reveal what he nearly broke a tooth on. A finger. An actual bloody finger.

'Dad planned out everything. He knew he wasn't going to be around to see this moment, so he asked me to literally give you the finger on his behalf.'

Charlie's mind flashes back to the body in the coffin. The leather gloves. Something that didn't quite look right. The slightly deflated gloved middle finger. Less prominent that the rest because the bloody thing had been removed, and deep fried. Served up like a sausage.

'And the best part is, there are plenty more bodies under there that people want to stay buried. How do you think I persuaded the other London families to look the other way while you waltzed in here?'

He looks left and right, disbelief that this is going down in the middle of a bloody wake, but the room behind him is emptying fast. His eyes flick from her to Logan Baird's finger, and back again, bile rising at the thought of that thing in his mouth. The hands holding him grip tighter, another reaching around, pinching his nose, tilting his head back. He gasps for air, mouth flopping open like a fish.

Ailsa Baird stands up, blue eyes as hard and cold as Arctic ice. The finger points.

'We've got something special planned for you, Charlie. Not just yet though. You've got to finish your dinner first. Eat up.'

*Copyright © 2023 Robert Scragg*

Robert Scragg had a random mix of jobs before taking the dive into crime writing. He's been a bookseller, pizza deliverer, karate instructor, football coach, and HR manager. He lives on the North East Coast with his wife, children and overly needy dog, and is a founding member of the Northern Crime Syndicate crime-writers group.

*What Falls Between the Crack*s, the first in his Porter & Styles series, was a New Writing North pick as one of the 2019 Read Regional books of the year. Rob's work has also seen him win the Lindisfarne Prize for Crime Fiction in 2021, as well as shortlisted for a CWA Dagger in 2021 and 2022.

# BOX

## CHRIS MCGEORGE

Daxx Narwhal died in front of 2.1 million people. Having survived for almost two weeks 250 metres underwater with no air, food or water, his glass box became his tomb. The cameras caught the entire incident.

'Really, this all hinges upon how he did it,' Ivan Drescher said. We were sitting in his Soho flat. He was musing over tea and custard creams. He had not offered me anything. 'We cannot attempt to hypothesise about how someone may have murdered Narwhal before we have ascertained how he stayed alive.'

The live feed of the event had been cut, but everyone saw. Millions of videos surfaced online, for anyone who hadn't been there at the time. The moment Narwhal perished had been viewed over 100 million times. Spikes in the video data showed the most replayed moments - his face turning puce, his eyes bulging to an almost comical size, his fingernails raking at his neck. By far the most replayed moment, however, was his face changing, his eyes, his cold realisation that this was finally, and fundamentally, *it*.

'Cyanide?' Drescher said, poring over the footage on my tablet.

With the cameras off, the glass box had been brought to the surface with remarkable speed. A post-mortem was performed. It was indeed cyanide.

'Ingested orally,' I said. Ever since I had been given the case, my cadence had become rigid, icy, wrong. My youngest had asked Mummy to read bedtime stories from now on. 'Thing is, we've sifted through all the footage and he doesn't once put anything in his mouth.'

'Curious.' Ivan Drescher had revealed himself to be something of an expert in impossible crimes during the investigation of the Soham Stranger. Although the solution of the case was attributed to me – the case that made my career – I honestly couldn't have done it without him.

Drescher was an outside consultant. He didn't have to help if he didn't wish to. From his puzzled expression however, I could tell his interest was piqued.

'I have never worked a locked-room case before, for the simple reason that they don't often appear. These are not the pages of Doyle, or Christie, or Poe after all. People kill people and often it is the least cunning way possible. The real world is rather dull in that regard.'

Daxx Narwhal did not live in the real world. For starters, Daxx Narwhal (surprising no one) was not his real name – although for the purposes of this account I will continue to call him such.

Narwhal grew up in Plymouth in the 90s. 'Daxx was a flamboyant child – a showman,' his Year 7 form teacher told a documentary crew after his first big break. 'If he could turn a situation into a smile on your face, he would. Even at personal cost. I suppose that's why he took the path he did.'

Narwhal stopped attending school as soon as he could – working at his father's construction business during the days and wandering the streets of Plymouth at night performing street magic for anyone with pocket change. His signature trick was one that did not pay off until days after an encounter with him when you'd find a playing card in the most unlikely place – the exact card you'd thought of in your head whilst staring into Narwhal's eyes. Narwhal never revealed how he did it, and now he never would.

He progressed into live theatre. From there, there were television deals, books, TIME magazine articles, late night chat shows. Narwhal became wildly successful in an incredibly short space of time. He bought himself a Los Angeles mansion.

He stopped calling himself a magician. He started calling himself an artist.

The shows became louder, longer, more aggressive. There was less audience participation. The lights were always on Narwhal.

'You seen the one where he shoots himself in the face?' aspiring magician Trevor Temor told me, before I conceded that I might need Drescher's assistance. Narwhal mentored him for two years. Temor had insights into Narwhal other people could only dream of. 'Who am I kidding? Of course you've seen it. The whole world did – before the clip got banned everywhere.' Narwhal's live show entitled *FATHOM* now exists only in the minds of the people who were there – and in the darkest corners of the Dark Web. 'He loads a bullet into that gun. He holds the gun up to his face. Not his temple, not his forehead – his face. And he pulls the trigger. The gun fires. The lights in the theatre go out. But for a split second, I see it. I see his head explode. Then the lights come up and he's as right as rain. A fun trick, huh? Except I feel a wetness on my cheek. I'm spattered in his blood and he's dancing around on stage without so much as a papercut.'

There were more of these 'stunts' – some recorded television specials, and some in front of a live audience. In *The Grand National* Narwhal lay down in front of a group of rampaging horses. *Freefall* saw Narwhal boarding an elevator on the top floor of a skyscraper and plummeting seventy-seven floors. In *Speed of Sound* he withstood three hours at top speeds in a supercharged G-force machine. There were more – many more.

Some stunts blurred the lines of fiction and reality. Narwhal took an interest in pilot training – completely outside of his illusionist career. On his first solo flight in Austria, his plane crashed into the mountains near the town of Ellmau. Narwhal climbed out of the burning wreckage with naught but a scratch on his cheek. The moment was captured by the iPhone of a man out walking his dog in the early morning dew. Narwhal stalked towards him with purpose; it seemed there was going to be some kind of incident, but Narwhal kept going, past him, into the forest, uttering only four words to the camera.

'Are you happy now?'

His motto. His sign-off.

It was how Narwhal ended every one of his shows. An earnest question to the audience – the only time all the showmanship, all the lights and the sounds and the music, all the 'pizzazz' fell away. A glimpse inside the Daxx Narwhal shell.

I had to explain all of this to Drescher. He didn't own a television. He had never heard of Daxx Narwhal before. It was a shame – by all accounts it seemed like Drescher and Narwhal would have got along. They were both secretive individuals, driven by a singular purpose – Drescher's was the discovery of truth, whilst Narwhal's was the obscuration of it. It would have proved an interesting dynamic.

'It seems he wanted to appear unkillable.'

Drescher was troubled by this. 'When one declares oneself immortal, others may see that as a challenge.'

\* \* \*

As I navigated our way through early morning London traffic, Drescher drew invisible diagrams on the dashboard. 'Locked-room mysteries always appear complex but are in most ways very simple. A person dies inside a locked room – how? There are a finite number of rational solutions. The simplest is obviously suicide.'

'But we have documented proof – 295 hours of livestream footage – that Narwhal couldn't have poisoned himself.'

'This footage has been verified, yes? We know it was not being digitally altered in any way.' Drescher and I were the old guard – hailing from the days where what was seen could generally be believed.

'The facts in front of us – as baffling as they appear – are correct. He got into that box. It was lowered slowly down to 250 metres underwater. He stayed there for 13 days, before he collapsed and died due to cyanide poisoning. Everything – everything – was on camera. Techs looked through all the footage and it's genuine. No cuts, or outages, or tricks. Now can you please tell me where we're going?' London was a rabbit warren with a flowing current.

I thought Drescher ignored me at first. 'We must take suicide off the table for now then. So we return to our next possible solution for a locked-room murder.'

'Which is?'

'Someone had a key.'

Drescher was standing in the box, surveying every detail. The box had been taken back to its birthplace – Beshmel Designs – as the evidence lockup back at the station hadn't really been built with something so large in mind.

The box.

Mr Luke Beshmel himself came to meet us. A big empty warehouse with naught but us in the middle. The box was being given the VIP treatment. 'My father started this company with the intention to provide immaculate and decadent display cases with departments in glass, acrylics, plastics and polymers. It was only after I came into the company that we pivoted towards something more ... eccentric.' Luke Beshmel was an engineer. A very good one. He worked on submarines, underwater bases, anything below sea level. 'I've always been fascinated with what's down there. I'm not talking about fish, or sharks, or squid. I'm talking about down there – the furthest one can go.'

There was a rapping on glass, and an annoyed face peering out at us. 'Can you please both keep it down?'

Beshmel seemed perplexed by this. 'The acrylic is so thick it's a wonder he can hear us.'

Drescher viewed the world differently to the rest of us – like through a television with all the settings turned to maximum.

'What's that?' I pointed to a unit on the south wall of the box.

'My pride and joy. Adapted it from submarine tech. Takes water and makes oxygen out of it. It's a process called electrolysis. Left side of that contraption is the oxygen generator. Right side is tasked with filtering out the carbon dioxide Narwhal created.'

'So Narwhal had a fresh supply of air.' I may have sounded disgusted. I supposed I was. He lied about the trick – in some capacity anyway.

'He didn't want the machine attached to the box. But he couldn't get round the fact that humans need to breathe. And whether he liked it or not, he was a human. Just like the rest of us.'

Beshmel grew silent, reflective. The cause of death hadn't been released to the public. Beshmel thought that he himself had killed Narwhal. Maybe, in some way, in going along with this whole cursed escapade, he had. But I didn't see how an air filtration unit killed Narwhal. In fact, it kept him alive.

I couldn't tell him. I wanted to, but I couldn't.

'There are no...' I had to find the formal word. '...facilities.'

'Well, he wasn't eating or drinking, so no need,'

Beshmel said. 'He told me his body would be completely free of any waste by the time he entered the box.'

Drescher was jumping up and down in the box, testing the floor.

'Anything else – call me.' I gave Beshmel my card, although he already had at least three.

\* \* \*

Daxx Narwhal lived on the screen. Everyone we interviewed said that he became someone else when he had an audience. As his fame grew, he tried more and more to be Daxx Narwhal and less and less the poor boy from Plymouth – as if he were afraid of being alone.

Viewing it all in retrospect, it was always going to be a self-fulfilling prophecy.

'He was so excited when he told me the idea – 'Underwater, Oli! Underwater!' he'd say. And I'd just look at him like he was mad and think how in the hell is he going to...'

'Shhh,' hissed Drescher.

Oliver Franklyn, Narwhal's manager and producer, was quiet. We were watching the raw footage from the documentary *BOX* – a documentary that now had a very different ending.

Onscreen, Narwhal was gearing up for a take. 'What awaits me inside the box? How long can I last with no air, no food, no water. Total solitude, unless you count the fish. Will I survive? Will I go insane? Will I emerge as something different, something evolved?'

'He didn't love all this documentary stuff,' Oliver said – a tentative glance at Drescher. 'The idea that you could get something wrong and just do it over. He did it –

danced our tune, but he thought it fake. He liked to do everything just once – like life, he said. He was built for the stage, the streets. He was built for the box.'

'Narwhal really didn't eat or drink whilst in there?' I asked.

'No. You can see on the cameras.'

'What was the trick?'

'If there was a trick, I am not privy to it.' As producer, Franklyn was facing charges of manslaughter and negligence. Given this, I couldn't help but think he was telling the truth. 'If these events, these stunts, were puzzles, Daxx never told a soul the solution. No one had the key to the mystery box.'

Drescher and I shared a look. Interesting terminology.

Franklyn mistook it. 'I know you both probably think me a fool – putting trust in this man. You never met him.'

Franklyn gave us remote access to the servers.

'You've got all the footage there. And every angle of the box. To watch it all would be an endurance feat in itself – I don't envy you.'

'What do you think happened down there?' I asked, as he escorted us out of the production office.

He shook his head. 'I think Daxx became something different – just like he said.'

Drescher didn't appear to be listening. He was transfixed by a seven foot cut-out of the man himself.

* * *

We made one final stop that day. I wanted Drescher to meet Trevor Temor, Narwhal's mentee. It was a mistake.

Oliver Franklyn pointed us to where Temor would be.

The production company mandated therapy for all their clients. The therapist's office was just around the corner.

Temor met us in the waiting room.

'This is Ivan Drescher – he's assisting in the investigation.'

Nods were exchanged.

Temor let us sit in on his therapy session, much to the chagrin of Steiner, his classic rendition of an elderly male therapist. If he were on the page, he'd be labelled lazy writing.

As Temor's session concluded, the conversation came onto Narwhal and the box. As Temor talked, I realised that he was indeed a great magician. Temor was planning his first large stunt himself. A jump into the Thames, from London Bridge. The details had not been finalised – and he was looking at ways to make it a risk assessor's nightmare.

Temor came alive when he talked of his impending dive into wavering mortality. I finally saw a man with passion. And passion could kill.

I asked a sole question to the therapist as we left. 'Narwhal ended every show, every special, every trick he performed with a question. "Are you happy now?? Did he ever reveal what this was about?'

We got a classic theory – one that we didn't need to pay a thousand pounds a session for. 'It was most likely directed towards his father,' Steiner said.

I managed to suppress the rolling of the eyes.

Drescher did not.

Before we parted with Temor, I asked the illusionist about his passion. 'Did you ever see Narwhal as competition?'

Temor laughed at this. 'Impossible. He was in a different league.'

'How would you do it? How would you poison a man inside a box 250 metres underwater?'

Temor didn't have an answer. 'Daxx existed in the unknown. He taught me a few things, yes, but nowhere near everything. It's the same with any profession. You can have it – the gene, or the knack, or whatever. I have it for illusion, yes. But Daxx had it more than anyone else I've ever known.'

'Both of you seem to share the idea of living life on the edge. Doing things others wouldn't dream of. Could that extend to killing another?'

Temor was troubled by this. Naturally. 'Why would I kill my friend?'

'Maybe you were jealous of him.'

Drescher laughed harder than Temor.

He undermined me. He knew it. If he was my Sergeant, maybe I'd have had his badge. As it stood, there was no real reason to bring it up. 'Temor is street-level,' Drescher explained, back in the passenger seat. 'You were correct, in certain areas. He's so wildly jealous of Narwhal that he's terrified of him. He doesn't even have the capacity to think of murdering Narwhal. One – he doesn't have the ability, and two – who thinks they can murder their God?'

I dropped Drescher off at his flat. I gave him copies of the footage. He stood out on the pavement expectantly, so I gave him my tablet computer as well. 'You should really join us all in the 21$^{st}$ century,' I said.

'Oh yes, because it looks like you're all having such a great time.'

If it wasn't said with such sincerity, I'd think he was attempting a joke.

\* \* \*

I didn't see Ivan Drescher for another three weeks. I called on him a few times, but there was no answer. The investigation was long but fruitless. I met so many faces, made so many connections, discounted so many potential motives that it all became somewhat of a blur. Was Narwhal cut down by his ex-manager, who he cut out of a lucrative deal? What about a scorned ex-lover who was left at an altar while Narwhal went to Africa to see if he could set up a stunt where he lived with a pride of lions? No – then how about a friend from childhood who turned out to be no friend at all but in fact the recipient of relentless bullying at Narwhal's hand.

I could go into more detail on these suspects, but it would only serve to be a waste of time – simply because it was a waste of mine.

In the wider world, the secret was out. A newspaper had obtained information that Narwhal had been poisoned with cyanide. My face was linked to the investigation. Everyone was talking about it. I couldn't go anywhere without people stopping me to ask if I had solved the great mystery of Narwhal and the Box. Some were nice when I told them I couldn't comment. Some were not.

Photographers followed me around like I was a celebrity.

For a brief period, Narwhal's face was replaced by mine on the front of every paper. My past success rate was dug up – of which I wasn't proud. I became a punchline. Jimmy Fallon joked about me in his opening monologue.

And then there were those who thought Narwhal was still alive, that this was all part of the trick.

With every passing hour, I saw this investigation for what it was.

This was never an investigation of motive. It was an investigation of opportunity. There was no opportunity. Maybe I had overstepped by accusing Temor because my subconscious had already known – this was beyond me.

So it was that I returned to the doorstep of a Soho flat on a windy Tuesday morning. The relief I felt when Drescher answered my knock was hopefully not shown on my face.

'I've watched it. All of it. Twice.'

'All of it?'

'Twice.'

He thrust my tablet at me.

I saw, with some amusement, that in a quiet moment Drescher had found his way to downloading Angry Birds.

He jabbed at the video player. 'Watch this.'

Footage of Narwhal preparing for the descent in the box. He was getting into the wetsuit he would be in for the remainder of his life. The wetsuit was purely for show – that and warmth.

'What's that there? He puts something in his mouth.'

Drescher was correct. Oliver Franklyn was standing next to Narwhal.

It wasn't a long journey to ask Franklyn.

'Yes, I remember that,' he said, confronted with the footage. 'I asked Daxx what he wanted his last meal to be

– before he went in. He simply pulled out a bit of gum – and already chewed at that.'

'Gum?' Drescher said. Even his usual monotone betrayed disappointment.

'Yes. Sorry – it was so trivial I forgot to mention it.'

Another dead end in an investigation full of them.

The car ride back was cold, and silent. Until...

'Gum,' Drescher said. 'You've heard the myth of gum taking seven years to digest in the human body?'

'Yes of course.' I didn't add that I did not know it was a myth and still thought it to be true.

'Poppycock of course – gum is usually fully digested inside of a week. But if it could be altered...'

'You're saying...?'

'Plastics and polymers.'

'Narwhal was interested in our other departments, yes,' Luke Beshmel said, as we visited him again. 'Particularly the one you mentioned. I gave him the design for a slow-release nutrient capsule that we could have easily developed there. The only issue would have been keeping the capsule inside the body for an extended period of time. Making sure it wasn't ... disposed of, by our body's natural impulses. Daxx was having none of it though. He saw it as cheating. So development was halted.'

'He saw the blueprints for this design?'

'Yes.'

'How would you have resolved the issue of keeping it inside the body?'

'We would have had to have made some way of slowing the capsule through the digestive tract. An abnormal shape, maybe. Or, a surface that would attach to the inner stomach — slow the process of digestion. Like...'

'Gum,' finished Drescher.

The work was not finished, and we were not done. The more we researched this avenue, however, the more it made sense. With this new found knowledge, we found that Narwhal had his own team — outside of Beshmel. He had history of cutting people out of decisions — just like with his ex-manager.

We interviewed members of his team. We uncovered the tests and the blueprints and the samples. None of them knew that Narwhal had taken this idea, and actually developed it.

A slow-release nutrient capsule that could be concealed in a sticky membrane of chewed gum. The capsule housed an inner core – once the nutrients had dissolved and the core was broken into, it would release its contents in a matter of seconds.

He must have done it alone, the team said. For what it was worth, I believed them.

Drescher grew triumphant.

I, however, grew troubled. I did not voice it, until Drescher left the station one day, and made his definitive goodbyes.

I couldn't help but stand there and watch as my unlikely partner started away. 'That's it? We're finished?' Drescher turned and I saw a desperate man reflected in his spectacles. 'We don't know if the polymer was successful. We don't even really know if it was real.'

Drescher stalked back. 'I apologise, but your level of satisfaction is beyond my concern. You came to me for an answer and now you have one. If it doesn't sit with you, I have nothing else to offer. My work is done.'

'So Narwhal killed himself? Why?'

Drescher smiled at this. 'So you would ask the question.'

'I don't...'

'Well ... I doubt we shall meet again.' It was abrupt.

Of course, I did indeed see Drescher again, albeit with myself wearing a different badge and himself wearing a different name. Alas, that is a story for another day. The case of the mystery box was solved adequately – officials were happy (indeed, almost too happy) to declare Narwhal's death suicide. To this day, I still wonder why he did it ... and I still wonder what I am truly wondering about. Drescher's final words on the subject have always stayed with me – the long looming shadow of Daxx Narwhal.

'You see, Ernst, this is precisely what was intended. Narwhal performed so many tricks where he survived, that it became a greater trick for him to perish.' He offered me his final thoughts as if appeasing a crying child, but it was his last remark before he turned away that chilled me.

'Are you happy now?'

\* \* \*

*Copyright 2023 Chris McGeorge*

\* \* \*

Chris McGeorge grew up in Norfolk, always wanting to create. He started writing comics about his favourite characters, progressing on to short stories. At school, he focused on English and wrote his first short story collection (mercifully unpublished) at 13.

He is a lover of Golden Age crime, such as Christie and Conan Doyle, leading his stories to be a mix of the old and the contemporary. He likes weird and wonderful plots, with plenty of intrigue and twists.

He studied an MA in Creative Writing (Crime/Thriller) at City University London, where he wrote his first novel as his thesis. His interests are broad – spanning film, books, theatre and video games. He is a member of the Northern Crime Syndicate, a supergroup of writers living in Northern England.

He lives in County Durham with his partner and many, many animals.

# DRIVE BY

## DG PENNY

The traffic is as bad as it gets. I'm blocked in by cars both right and left. For a moment paranoia fills me. Memories of Helmand. Out there, you always needed space. An escape route.

I return to the present, grateful for the driver behind when he sounds his horn. I lurch forward twenty feet and stop again. I look across to the other lanes beyond the central barrier. The cars there aren't moving either, but beyond them, on the grass verge, a van has pulled off the road. Another flashback fills my head. A broken-down pickup truck with men standing around it. Innocent enough, except we've seen it all before. AKs waiting in the back of the truck. Maybe a homemade bomb. But this is London. This is England. It's not Afghanistan. Not yet.

There are three men beside the van and a young girl. Fifteen pretending to be twenty-one. Short skirt. Short top. Small breasts. Long hair. She's pretty in an ordinary way. I glance ahead but nothing's moving. People stand beside their cars trying to see what the hold-up is.

Then one of the men grabs the girl by the hair and slams her head into the side of the van.

She doesn't make a sound.

Adrenaline floods through me even though I know this isn't my fight.

I try to look away, then glance around at the other people in their cars. Nobody else appears to have seen what happened. No one reacts.

Another of the three men pushes her against the van and leans in close. He says something that doesn't carry over the sound of cars. Then he slaps her face.

Still nobody reacts.

I open my door and step out because it's what I've been trained to do. See trouble, sort it. Just like they say at train stations. But our way of sorting was a different kind. This country spent a lot of money on me. Taught me how to see danger. Taught me how to deal with it. I've done it all and wish I could forget most of it, but I can't. It keeps coming back. Late at night lying beside Jen with a cold sweat on my back as I listen to her breathing. Listening ... listening ... hearing the distant sound of gunfire and the screams of men dying in agony.

Now the girl screams and one of the men slaps her into silence.

I don't even think. I'm over the barrier and in the other lane before I even know I'm going to do it. Faces stare out at me through windscreens, wondering who the idiot is. They've seen nothing. So who's the idiot — me or them?

Then I'm there, with the men.

"Leave her alone." I try for calm but firm.

One of them turns to me. Pale skinned. East European,

but which part of east Europe I can't tell. Sometimes white folk all look the same.

"Fuck off. This is nothing to do with you." He has an accent, but I can't place that either.

I reach out to the girl. "I can't do that, man. I'm taking her with me."

Two of the men laugh. The third takes a swing.

I duck under it, then my hand snaps out, not hard, a slap, nothing more, but he takes a step back. Surprised. Not used to someone fighting back. More used to young women and scared men. I've seen his kind before. Then I discover these men are different.

Hard men. Arrogant men. Out of control and used to getting their own way. Arms grab me from behind, pinning my own to my sides. The man I slapped throws a punch which connects to the side of my head, sending it snapping around. Lights flash and the world spins away. I feel my legs go loose and try to fight it, but another punch is on its way. I manage to avoid it by stepping back, putting my heels down on the toes of the guy holding me. My work shoes with solid heels. He releases his hold. I lash out. Two fast punches, no slaps now. These are meant to do damage, but the man who hit me is also hard and stops one. The other gets through.

He shakes his head and punches out again. This time I manage to deflect. I kick out, aiming for his knee which snaps backwards and he limps to one side. I sense the others coming up behind me and spin around. Two punches, one for each, then I grab the girl and run out into the road just as the traffic starts to move again.

Horns blare. Windows come down and voices curse at me. Everyone's more concerned about being late for work than a girl in trouble. People on one side of the dual carriageway going somewhere. People on the other going somewhere else. It always occurs to me they ought to swap houses and save the commute, but I guess that's too logical.

The girl drags along beside me, not helping.

My car door is still open, but the other cars are swerving around it. Swerving around me and the girl as I pull her to the far side and throw her into the passenger seat. I run back around. As I glance across the road I see the three men coming after me. The glint of something bright held in one of their hands. Something dark in the other that might be a gun.

I floor the accelerator and pull away, getting a barrage of horns from behind.

Then I'm gone, heart beating fast, sweat pooling under my shirt. I glance at the girl but she's curled around herself, arms across her belly, hair hiding her face.

"Put your seat belt on," I say, but she doesn't move. It's not the worst thing that might happen to her. "What did those men want?"

This time she might shake her head. It moves, but that could be from the potholes in the road.

I take a left then a right. On back roads now, still busy but fewer cars because there are fewer lanes. As I slow for lights she moves suddenly and grabs the door handle. She wants out, but I reach across and drag her back. I press the button to lock all the doors. Child locks, they call them, and close up she's barely more than a child.

"What's your name?"

No response.

"I'm Dean," I say. "Dean Carter."

Still nothing from her.

I glance in the rearview mirror as the lights change and see a white van six cars back, three men lined across the seats. They must have bullied their way through traffic and now they're behind me.

I take another left and the van follows. Nothing between us now. I'm headed down a narrow street and at the end of it lies the Thames. A dead end. Almost.

An even narrower roadway runs off left and right. This time I go right. Pontoons on the river. Multi-million-pound houses on the other side of the road. Beyond the churning river a park. I recognise where we are and put my foot down. Dog walkers leap aside. A woman pushing a pram tries to play hardball then chickens out when she sees I'm not going to stop. I'd have hit her except I go onto the kerb, then jerk the wheel hard to bring me back because there are two kids on their way to school, smart uniforms and leather satchels. They look like they've tele-ported in from the 1950s, except they'll have names nobody used back then, names like Tamsin and Jeremy.

The van is still behind me so I lurch along the next road, then left, right again and I'm almost on Hammer-smith flyover, the brewery on my right. I drop down to the roundabout, skid around it, fly through red lights and streak past the Apollo where I saw John Hiatt play a killer set a few years back.

I've lost the van.

Past Hammersmith Hospital. Over Putney Bridge. Another side road and I pull up in a parking lot where the ground is bare dirt. I kill the engine and turn to the girl.

Now she looks up. Scoops hair back from her face. She's pretty, the left side of her face red from where the man slapped her. Pale grey eyes. Red lipstick on lips that look too young for such a colour.

She reaches out for me. Her hand goes to my fly and she says, "You want I blow you now?"

I jerk away. "What? Of course not."

"I give good head," she says. Her accent is East European, like the men. I imagine her being promised the world. Money. Fame. A career.

"Who are they?"

"Nobody."

"So what did they want with you?"

"Nothing."

I glance at my watch. Nine-thirty Thursday morning. I'm already late for work and my boss will be pissed off. I think of calling in with some excuse but know it won't make a damn bit of difference. Instead, I reach across and pull the seat belt across the girl and leave the parking lot.

When I pull the car into the drive at home and go inside my hand is grasping the girl around the wrist. Dark fingers around chalk-pale skin. Jen's not there. I smell her perfume, but she's gone out. She'll have dropped Cally at school but is usually back by now. At least I assume she should be, but I don't know what she does with her day. She works from home. One of those new jobs where you only meet your colleagues once a month. Maybe less.

"You goin' to fuck me now?" says the girl.

"What's your name?"

"What you wan' it to be, mister? I can be whoever you wan'."

I don't know what to do with her. Don't know what I was thinking. Except I wasn't thinking. I reacted. Like I'd been trained to do.

I go to the window and look out. The row of houses across the street are mirror images of those on my side. When I turn back the girl's removed her top and is smiling at me, coming forward. She has small breasts, and I wonder again how old she is. Not old enough for this.

"They make you do it, don't they?" I say.

The grin is still on her face as she shakes her head. "I like to do it. Like big men like you. Black men. You got a big dick, too?"

I pick up her top and struggle her back into it. This is a mistake. And then I hear a key in the door and Jen comes in.

She stops and stares at us, a shopping bag in her left hand.

"What's going on, Dean? Who is this?"

I shake my head, searching for an answer. I know what she's thinking.

"I saved her from a beating," I say.

"Why?"

Good question.

"I had to. Three men were trying to get her into the back of a white van."

"Is the colour significant?" Jen walks into the kitchen and unloads her shopping. An avocado. Bottle of white wine. Sourdough bread from the deli. Pate. Sliced meat. Her lunch, perhaps. Even the wine.

She turns to the girl. "What's your name, sweetie?" It seems even she thinks the girl's too young.

She gets no response and turns to me. "What are you going to do with her, Dean?"

"I don't know."

"There are services, aren't there? The council? The

police?" She nods to the hallway where our never used hard-wired phone sits. "You should call them."

"I need the bathroom," the girl says.

Jen's face is a mask of panic.

"There's one at the end of the hall," I say.

"No," says Jen, "I'll take her upstairs. She might want a shower or something." She gives me a look and mimes dialling, even though nobody actually dials anymore. She wants me to ring while the girl is out of the way.

It makes sense. The trouble is, who do I call? I don't know any services other than the obvious. I use my mobile and punch in three nines.

"What service do you require?"

"Police."

The call is transferred and picked up. I tell someone what's happened. A girl being abducted. Someone takes my details. I tell them I don't know what to do.

"Stay where you are, we'll send someone to see you as soon as we can. Thank you, Mr Carter."

When I turn around Jen is watching me.

"Where is she?"

"In the bathroom."

"I'm sorry," I say. "I couldn't ignore what was happening."

Jen shakes her head. "It's just like you, Dean. For all the hard-man image you're a soft touch." She smiles and comes across the room. I hug her. Smell that scent of hers I love.

When we pull back, Jen says, "You called someone?"

"The police. They're sending someone around."

She looks past me. "That might be them now."

When I turn, I see a white van pull up at the bottom of our drive, blocking my car in.

"Go out the back way," I say. "Through the gate and along the footpath. Go to the coffee shop at the end of the road and stay there until I come to find you."

"What?" Jen stares past me, her face paling.

"Do it now. There's no time to argue." I push her away and she walks backwards before turning and walking fast to the back door.

I go upstairs. The bathroom door is locked. I knock but get no response. I put my shoulder against it and the slim lock gives. The girl has the wall cabinet open and has taken out bottles of pills from inside. Some to help Jen sleep. A few stronger ones from when my body was healing.

I can't tell if she's taken any.

I hear knocking on the front door, then something smashing against it.

There's no time, so I grab the girl and drag her out and downstairs. I follow Jen to the back door as the front one crashes open.

I push the girl ahead of me, her feet stumbling, and I see she's taken her pumps off and is barefoot. I throw her out through the back door. Grab the key, slam the door and lock it. It might hold them for half a minute. I grab her again and we go out the back gate. I have no idea how they knew where to find me. Could they have traced my car?

"Who are those men?" I say as we stumble and trip along the footpath.

Mrs Stevenson from 42 comes towards us with her

pug pulling her along on its lead. She stares at me, then looks away. She doesn't want to get involved.

"Gangsters," says the girl. It's the first sensible answer she's given since I took her away from them. "You don't want to cross them. Bad men. Very bad men. They kill you." The second sensible answer, but it's too late.

At the end of the road, I see a police car turn the corner. As it approaches I step into the road and wave my arms. I feel like an idiot, but they stop.

A woman gets out, settling her cap on her head. "I'm sorry sir; you need to let us pass."

"It was me who called you," I say. "This is the girl. And there are men in my house and a van outside it. They're bad men." I parrot the girl. "Very bad men."

She looks at me. At the girl. Then she thumbs her radio.

"Four-one-seven requesting assistance. Possible abduction." She rolls off my address and then turns back to me. "Please, sir, get in the car. You too, miss."

"He raped me," she says, taking a step away. She raises her arm and points at me. "This man raped me. My friends have come for me."

"Shit," says the policewoman. She leans over and knocks on the car window. "I need you, Frank. Get your arse out here now."

She reaches for the girl's arm but she darts away and sets off down the road. The woman starts after her.

"She might have taken some tablets," I call out, but if she hears me she doesn't react.

"Now then, sir, can you tell me exactly what is happening here?"

I'm saved from coming up with an answer, either the

truth or something more believable, by the appearance of the white van. It rounds the corner from my street and idles for a moment. I can see the three men in the front. Then it starts forward, accelerating hard. It comes directly at me. At us.

I wait, knowing if I move too soon they'll swerve. So I wait some more. The van is close. Maybe too close.

I grab the constable and throw him to one side, then myself the other way.

The van weaves, undecided. I roll away, hearing the screech of metal behind me. Then the van is slowing. It starts to back up, but in the distance I hear sirens. The policewoman's call has borne fruit. Reinforcements are on the way.

The men in the van must hear it too, but still they keep coming.

One of them leans out the window, looking directly at me. His hand comes out, holding a gun.

He fires. Three shots in quick succession, but all of them miss. Pistols are useless. I know from experience. If you want to hit someone you can't beat a rifle.

Two police cars screech into the street, and finally, the van driver decides to take the sensible option. Well, kind of sensible. He floors the accelerator and aims for the tiny gap between them. Both cars swerve out of the way and the van crashes through the too-small gap, taking both wing mirrors with it. At the end of the road it squeals around the turn and is gone. One of the damaged cars does a three-point turn and sets off in pursuit. The other decants four armed men who march toward me.

I put my hands on top of my head, kneel and wait.

* * *

The interview room is nicer than I expect. The two police sitting opposite me less so.

"Explain it to me again, Mr Carter. How you took the girl."

"I didn't take her," I say. "I rescued her."

"The other men we took into custody tell a different story. They say..." the female detective glances at a sheaf of notes that had been brought in only five minutes before, "...that you kidnapped the girl and drove off."

"Yes, I took her. Yes, I drove off. But they were beating her. You've seen her bruises."

"Which she claims were made by you."

I stare at her, then glance at the man beside her. His face is expressionless. Not unfriendly, but not friendly either.

"They were pimping her out," I say. "She has to be underage."

"Her passport shows her as nineteen years old. One of the men says he is her uncle and corroborates that information."

I start to laugh, stop myself. "Then it's fake, and he's a liar. If they're innocent why did they drive off? Why did they crash into two of your cars? Why did they shoot at me?"

"We are talking to you in this room, Mr Carter. Other colleagues are speaking with the men. But I can tell you they say they were afraid you were about to attack them. We have found no sign of any weapon."

"And you believe all that?"

"At the moment we believe nothing. We are interviewing all those involved."

"They had a gun. Fired at me. Fired at your colleague."

"I told you, we found no gun."

"Of course not."

She glared at me, the first honest emotion I had seen from her. "Are you saying I'm lying, Mr Carter?"

"Of course not. I'm saying they tossed the gun."

"We took swabs from their hands and found no residue. Perhaps you thought you saw a gun."

"I spent three tours in Afghanistan. I know a gun when I see one."

She sighed and looked at the man. "Is she still outside?"

He nods.

She looks back at me. "Mr Carter, I believe this is something and nothing." She leans closer. "In fact, it's a shit-storm, and I don't like shit-storms. So I will tell you what I intend to do. Nobody's dead. Nobody's hurt — not even the girl. We had her checked out, of course. So I'm going to issue you with a warning. Do not approach the girl again. Do not approach the men again. In fact, I want you to stay away from white vans for a while too. If you agree and sign a statement to that effect I will release you. Your wife is waiting outside but says she has to leave soon to pick up your daughter." She stares at me. "So?"

I nod. "Show me where to sign."

* * *

It's a bunch of crap. I know it. They know it.

As I walk out of the police station beside Jen I see two

of the men standing across the road smoking cigarettes. There's no sign of the van. Their body language changes when they see me and I tense, preparing for an attack, but they stay where they are.

"Where are we parked?" I ask Jen.

"Waitrose. Probably going to get a ticket for over-staying."

Not the worst of our problems.

I'm already thinking. Planning ahead. Making a list of who to call. Trying to remember who's in the country and who is not.

"I want you to do something for me," I say.

Jen glances at me. "What — dress up like that little schoolgirl and play hard to get?"

I sigh, knowing whatever I say won't change her mind about what happened.

"I want you to take Cally to your mother's for the weekend."

"What if I have plans?"

"Do you?"

"Other than playing school with you?" This time she smiles and I see she's starting to come around to the notion none of this is my fault. Except it is my fault. All of it. Any normal man would have looked the other way and driven by.

"Please, Jen, humour me. Just the weekend. You can come back Sunday night and I'll cook you something delicious."

She just stares at me and I know I've gone too far.

"All right, a takeaway then. That Indian place you like."

"Flowers would be nice, too," she says.

I look back, but the men are gone. Only me and Jen walking to Waitrose, the ice between us thawing. It's going to take time but we'll get back to the old ways eventually.

"Don't say anything about this to Cally."

I don't want our daughter involved, but I see it's the wrong thing to say as soon as the words are out of my mouth. Jen gets into the car but leaves the passenger door locked. She starts up and drives away, almost running over my foot.

When she's gone from sight I take my phone out and start making calls.

Four of us sit in the living room at home. I figure four of us is enough. There are beers on the coffee table, as well as coffee, but no one touches the beer. We don't plan on getting drunk. It feels good to catch up, to talk shit about what we claim we did out there. Billy was my closest bud and it was him I called first. He said yes. Of course he did. Didn't even ask me what the trouble was. Garry wanted all the ins and outs, same as always. I told him to wait otherwise I'd have to tell it three times. I said the same to Mike. And now they know. About the girl. The men. The police. My warning.

"Do you think they'll come tonight?" asks Billy, his accent pure back street Glasgow. If I hadn't spent time with him I'd have no idea what he said.

"What would you do?" I ask.

"I'd come tonight. You know I would."

"Me too," says Mike. He's East End London, the old

East End that no longer exists, all tower blocks and dealers now but Mike never gets any trouble.

"It would've been good to get some hardware," says Garry in his broad Black Country voice. He holds a hand up. "I know, I know, best not, but still it would've been good. Put the fear of God into the bastards."

"Three, you said?" asks Billy.

"Three that I saw. That doesn't mean there won't be more."

"East European? Which part?"

I shrug. "East is all I know. There are some mad fuckers out there. And these are mad fuckers."

"And the girl? She'll be gone by now."

"Most likely. Moved on. Another town. Another bunch of creeps."

"So we've only got the mad fuckers to deal with," says Garry with a grin.

Just like old times. The heat of the day barely fading as the sun sets and we prepare our weapons for night patrol. Hoping we see action because that's why we're there. Who we are. All four of us and the others I couldn't reach. Sure, we wake in the night sometimes in a cold sweat, but none of us suffers like some we know. Here, in a suburban four-bed, two-garage, the sense of expectation is the same.

\* \* \*

They come at three in the morning. Of course they do. I wonder if they're military as well, somewhere in the past. One of those little wars most of us tried to ignore.

There are three of them, so perhaps there are no more. Which would be good.

Billy shakes me awake and tells me that with his fingers.

"Where?" I ask.

"One out back, two in front. They got into the garage and are working on the door into the house. It ain't gonna take them long after the last time. Mike's down there with Garry. I let you have a bit more beauty sleep seeing as you need it more than the rest of us." He grins.

I stand and reach for the baseball bat beside the bed, knowing as I feel its heft I could get arrested for possession of it. Fortunately, I also have a catcher's mitt and ball so can claim I play the game. Each of us carries something similar. Something familiar. None of us ever sleeps without something close to hand.

From the top of the stairs I can hear someone working the lock I only paid to be fixed a few hours before. I'll have to repair the damage again when we've dealt with them. One more negative in their ledger to go alongside the £50 fine for overstaying at the Waitrose car park. I told Jen I'd pay it. She said, "Of course you will."

As we descend the stairs Mike appears from the kitchen.

"The guy at the back's about to smash your door in with a sledgehammer, Deano. You want me to go out and take it off him before he does?"

"I'll do it," I say. "It's my door."

I go out a window at the side, glancing to one side as I do. One garage door is half-raised and I can hear cursing from inside. The white van is parked at the end of the road, one wheel on Mr Harding's lawn. I smile, thinking of the bollocking he'd give them if he saw it.

I go around and in through the side gate.

The man is standing in front of the door and I can see him tensing up ready to swing.

"Hey, that door's solid," I say, moving towards him. "Let me help."

He's fast. Turns to me, the hammer swinging my way. I'd be stupid to try and block it and get a broken arm or skull. Instead, I duck, hearing him grunt as the sledge-hammer goes above me. I grab an iron poppy head, one of six Jen has bought for the border. I turn it so the pointed bit is in my hand, then whack him hard on the side of the head. He drops the sledgehammer and cries out. Slaps his hand to his face where blood is welling. I move closer, move fast. I drop the iron poppy and use my fists. One to the side of the head. One to his solar plexus. Then I kick his knee out of place and he falls. I kick him again and he's out of the game. I snap zip ties round his wrists and ankles.

I unlock the back door and walk in just in time to see the side door to the garage open and two men rush in. Billy takes one with a huge uppercut and he goes back out faster than he came in. The other is grasped on either side by Garry and Mike. They drag him into the kitchen and sit him down.

I pull a chair up to the other side and select a knife from the wooden block.

"Now, we can do this the nice way or the messy way. Which is it to be?"

He spits at me.

Billy grasps his wrist and holds his hand out. I jab the

point of the knife down through the back of it and he screams. Seems he's not so hard after all. I twist the knife then pull it out.

"Now see," I say, "this is the nice way. You do not want to find out the alternative, do you?"

He spits again, so I stab him through his other hand.

"Look, you've made me mark this nice table. My wife is going to be angry. You do not want to make my wife angry, do you?"

This time he doesn't spit. His hands are clenching and unclenching, blood pooling beneath them.

"You're a dead man."

I look at the other three. "Do I look dead, boys?"

"As alive as ever," says Garry. "Can we put them in the van and torch it?"

I make it look like I'm considering the option before shaking my head.

"Too good for them."

"Push it in the river, then? Let it fill up slowly with water while they struggle?"

"We have friends," says the man. "They know we came here. Know who you are. Anything happens to us, and they come for you. More than three next time."

I look into his eyes and smile. "If you had friends you'd have brought them with you." I lean closer. "Who told you where I live?"

"We have our sources."

"In the police? DVLA? The council?"

"Fuck you."

"No, I don't think so."

I'm starting to get a bad feeling about this. These men should have the same kind of caution I do. If they were rational they would have walked away. Chalked it up to experience. Next time take it out on their girls away from the main road into North London. But these are not rational men. If I let them walk away they will come back. They may or may not have friends, but they will have money. Dirty money. It doesn't take much to hire killers in London. I glance at Billy, Garry and Mike. They will back me whatever I decide, then walk away without so much as a backward glance.

Fire. Water. Knife. Or fists and boots. I think about the gun one of them pointed at me and wonder if it's still somewhere in their van, or most likely they have another. If so, why didn't they bring it?

"Go search the others," I say to Mike.

He's gone four minutes, during which I stare at the man across the table from me. He stares back. Trying to look hard, but he can see something in my eyes he doesn't like. Something that scares him.

When Mike comes back he has the keys to the van.

"Bring it here," I say. "Back it up to the garage."

He goes out without a word.

I nod at Garry and Billy and they lift the man to his feet. He doesn't want to go, but between us we throw him in the back of the van. There are stained mattresses in there and it stinks of sweat and sex. We snap ties around his wrists and ankles, then do the same for the others.

As we drive them away I see Mr Harding's upstairs light come on and his curtains twitch. If the police come asking he'll tell them what he saw. A white van driving away.

I drop Garry and Mike off at the train station and hand

each an envelope of cash. They try to hand it back but I insist, and neither of them is stupid.

Billy sits beside me as we drive out of London, the roads quiet but never still.

"How far you want to go?" Billy asks.

"What you got in mind?"

"I know this place north of Glasgow," he says. "Isolated. Quiet. We leave them there and let whatever happens happen." He shakes his head. "You're too soft, Deano. Always have been. Remember that kid in Helmand? You said to leave him, and then he tossed a grenade."

"I'm not killing them," I say. "And you're not either."

Billy shrugs. "Fair enough. Besides, Glasgow's a fuck of a long drive from here."

"Not so far. Show me somewhere nice and quiet. Somewhere a white van can't be seen. Somewhere it might sit for a month or a year before it's found."

"I can do better than that, pal."

And he does. We leave the van sitting in a dry riverbed. Billy tells me it's a place that's either dry or a raging torrent after a storm.

We hear the sound of kicking as we climb the hillside back to the road. Dark clouds gather over the mountains and distant thunder sounds.

They say time heals. It can also kill.

* * *

* * *

David Penny is the author of the Thomas Berrington Historical Mysteries, set in the chaotic final years of Moorish al-Andalus in Spain and the early Tudor period in England. After having four science-fiction novels published in his 20s, he stopped writing for 40 years. When he took it up again, he chose to publish independently. David's work is available in eBook, print and audio, and also translated into Spanish and German.

David is working on *The Murder Trail*, a new police crime thriller series featuring DC Izzy Wilde, to be published under the pen name DG Penny.

# CREATURES OF THE NIGHT

## PAUL FINCH

It was somewhere around midnight when Kathy decided that she'd made a big mistake letting Michael camp out with his friends. She sat upright in bed, wondering what had possessed her. All right, there were three of them and Maybury Park was only round the corner, but they were only eleven years old, and it suddenly seemed horribly quiet out there.

She crossed the bedroom, pulled the drapes aside and looked out. How deserted the town was at this hour. Nothing moved. The yellow glow of the street lamps seemed to create more dark spaces than light ones: in gardens, under trees, in the many narrow ginnels linking one street to the next. Even the cars were immovable objects, sleek and gleaming, but filled with blackness, rooted to the kerb. Drawn curtains on the windows of neighbouring houses shut them off too, the beings inside unreachable in their voids of sleep. The stillness was tangible. Kathy imagined you could draw a knife through it and hear its fabric ripping.

She dithered for a moment. Michael would probably sulk for days. Not so much because he'd been denied a night's camping out, but because of the humiliation in the eyes of his school-friends. She wondered what Bill would have said, had he still been living at home. Probably something macho and empty-headed like, "this is the sort of things lads of his age get up to". Or "when I was a lad, we used to go camping in the Brecon Beacons never mind the town park". She could just picture him as he said it, slouched in front of the TV, beer in one hand, doorstep-thick bacon sarnie in the other, eyes fixed on the screen.

That decided her. She whipped her nightie off, climbed into her jeans, and pulled on a sweatshirt and an old pair of trainers. Anything her ex-husband thought okay was definitely a no-no. That path had always led to disaster.

It was a dry, clear night, but cool for September, so she put on her mac and scarf before venturing out. However, when she stepped from the porch, a new reservation struck her. It wasn't so much about her son's safety now, as her own. Since her divorce, two years ago, she had hardly ever been out at night, except at weekends, when the town was alive with revelers, and even then in the company of friends. A midweek night like this would be a different matter. More to the point, the house she and Michael lived in was large and detached, circled by extensive gardens. Access to Ashwood Lane was via the drive, which ran for twenty yards through trees and bushes. At this hour they were a formless leafy mass, offering many a dark place for any would-be attacker to hide.

Kathy hung back. She could always get the car out,

she supposed, but it hardly seemed worth it with the park only five minutes' walk away.

She steeled herself and went down to the road. This was a pretty safe neighbourhood. It was an official Home Watch area, and they were a long way from the town centre, where the more dangerous hooligans tended to hang out. If she couldn't just nip round the corner in safety, then society was really in trouble.

That said, for a major trunk road, Ashwood Lane was unnervingly quiet. It ran straight at this section, in either direction dwindling off into the distance, bereft of cars or pedestrians. She hovered at the bottom of the drive, gazing towards the nearest junction, which was about two hundred yards away and controlled by traffic lights. They changed as she watched, steadily and repeatedly. Monotonous, serving no one.

Spooky, that.

Determinedly, she walked the other way, coming quickly to the corner of Maybury Close. The park lay down at the far end. Kathy jammed her hands into her mac pockets, glancing over her shoulder before setting off down towards it.

And was forcibly stopped in her tracks.

Her heart skipped a beat.

For half a second then, way down Ashwood Lane, she fancied she'd seen the figure of a man stepping quickly into someone's driveway.

Kathy stood trembling. Had she or hadn't she? There was no sign of anyone now, but then there wouldn't be if he'd just ducked out of sight.

Kathy hurried on down Maybury Close. There'd be

nothing in it; whoever he was, he was probably just going home.

*Ducked out of sight,* indeed! More likely he'd just been entering his own drive.

Not that that explained the odd look of the man. Kathy tried to tell herself that she'd only glimpsed him momentarily, but she'd still been given the impression of a very long coat, ankle-length in fact, a briefcase and thick straggling hair hanging down over his back and shoulders. There'd also been a beard, she thought; a dark, unkempt beard. Kathy was certain of one thing, she knew of no one in this neighbourhood who looked like that. Still, it wasn't worth dwelling on. She looked over her shoulder as she walked.

Nobody had come round the corner after her, but she still felt a prickle of goosebumps.

She saw no one else and heard nothing more until she reached the bottom end of Maybury Close and crossed over to the park. A dull, distant light flickered far out in its pitch-black depths. Michael and his friends' tent.

Maybury Park wasn't a park as such. More an open green space between housing estates, planted with elm trees and the odd flowerbed. When Michael had first told her the plan, she'd never considered there could be any danger. They'd be surrounded by houses after all, but at this time of night they seemed a long way from anyone; the light was a minuscule pinpoint in dense shadows.

Kathy walked more quickly. The grass was soaked with dew and littered with early leaves. She realised that her breath was smoking. Then she wondered why she was rushing. Even when the tent's triangular shape came into view, she felt panic. The light was on inside, but it threw no shadows on the canvas. There were no sounds of horseplay or boyish laughter. Unavoidably, she started running. In front of the tent, she could see a litter of crisp bags and empty pop bottles.

Panting hard, she ripped the flap back and stuck her head inside.

All three of them were in there, curled up in their sleeping bags. Her sudden intrusion brought them awake with cries of fright. Then groans of disbelief.

"Michael," she said firmly. "Come on, please. We're going."

He was about to protest, but she gave him her hardest look, and sullenly, he commenced getting his stuff together. Kathy was surprised at the ease of her victory. She'd expected at least *some* resistance. As it was, he pulled on his anorak and hiking boots, and rolled his bits and pieces up in his sleeping bag. The other two boys watched him in silence, pop-eyed with sleep, faces chalk-white and sickly from unaccustomed exposure to the night air. Only when she closed the flap on them, did they talk, a furtive, mumbled conversation.

"Thanks mum," Michael said, stumping ahead of her. "I knew this would happen!" But he still didn't put up the real fight he was capable of.

Kathy thought she knew why. She glanced around. The trees were black stanchions silhouetted on the distant glow of the streetlights. Here under the elms, the shadows were thick, bottomless, making it difficult to see your own hand in front of your face. It was easy to think you'd be brave in the daylight hours, but things changed at night. Unwittingly, she'd given him the excuse he'd been looking for. It pleased her to have her authority reinforced by physical reality. Doubtless he'd never admit it though.

Then a flicker of movement caught her eye.

She stopped sharply, grabbing Michael's shoulder. He winced and pulled away and was about to say something, when he saw her expression. She was staring hard to their left, her eyes straining to penetrate the dark.

"What?" He rubbed his shoulder melodramatically.

"Nothing," she said in a tight voice. "Let's get on ... it's very late."

She was damned if she was going to tell him she thought she'd just seen someone sliding out of sight behind one of the tree-trunks. Fleetingly, the thought struck her that now it was wrong to leave the other two lads behind, but her motherly instincts were working full tilt. Getting Michael to home and safety first was a priority. She felt the urge to put an arm around his shoulders as they walked, but knew he'd shrug it off.

They reached the pavement without incident and hurried along it, but Kathy could sense that vast, unlit stretch of parkland behind them. The echoes of their footfalls seemed unnaturally loud. So loud that they'd surely never hear someone creeping up.

"Soon be home, now," Kathy said.

Michael grunted, as if that was all he needed.

It was only a five-minute walk away, but Kathy was now thinking about the numerous drives and gates they had to pass first, about the multiple parked cars and vans with the unseen niches between them, about the various low walls overhung with densely leafed branches. How little light the sodium-yellow lamps actually gave off when it came down to it. They were halfway up Maybury Close when a sudden violent *CRASH* sounded somewhere behind them. Both jumped and Kathy spun round.

She half hoped to see someone. Locking their car in a garage maybe, or putting the cat out of a side door. However, there was no one. Nor were there any tell-tale lights, either outside or inside any of the houses. Everywhere she looked, she saw drawn curtains. Her friends' and neighbours' impregnable barriers against the creatures of the night.

"Almost there," she told Michael again, hoping he wouldn't notice the shake in her voice. At which point, from the corner of her eye, she saw a face.

Waiting just around the side of a house.

Watching them with a hideous leering expression.

Kathy sucked air through clenched teeth. She tried not to scream.

And in that same instant realised that it was nothing more than a garden statue. A mossy stone cherub dancing in the middle of someone's back lawn, now framed in an open side gate. It was still curious, the sneery expression on its partly eroded face, the way it seemed to track them with its blank stone eyes as they passed.

"Why'd you come and get me?" Michael asked, not even having noticed it. "The others' mums aren't bothered."

"I just had second thoughts, that's all," Kathy replied.

"There's no-one else about, you know. I'm certain we'd be alright." He spoke in an irritable, patronising tone.

*Sure,* she thought. *We're almost back inside now. But it didn't take a wild horse to drag you away from that tent, did it.*

As they approached the corner with Ashwood Lane, Kathy slowed and stopped.

Michael regarded her curiously. "We waiting for a bus or something?"

"Just a minute!" Heart pounding, she edged to the corner and looked round it.

As before, the road was deserted, the ever-changing traffic light a sentinel shape at the far end. Their own drive was only fifty or so yards away, but now they were close to where she'd thought she'd seen that weird-looking bearded guy. Kathy realised that this was what she'd most feared all along: arriving back home. Whatever the atmospheric effects the midnight hour and the figments of her own imagination had contrived to do to her on the way to and from Maybury Park, getting back to Ashwood Lane was never going to have provided comfort, because she knew that there really *was* someone hanging around here.

But where was he now? Still down the far end? Or hiding a little closer?

As she waited and watched, Michael asked her what was wrong. She glanced down at him. He seemed genuinely puzzled, though in recent months the pleasing impishness of infancy had noticeably drained from his face, supplanted by a surly, pugnacious look, which she recognised from his father. Increasingly, it said: "Why do you women have to get under our feet all the time? Why do you have to make an issue of every little thing!"

How typical of Bill it would have been to regard caution as a weakness and simply go blundering in. Sooner or later, she'd have to break her son of that.

She glanced back along the road. It was still deserted.

The entrance to their own drive lay tantalisingly close. Their own drive ... with all those bushes and trees along it.

That would be an ordeal in itself.

"There's nothing here," he told her loudly. Now there was a note of real aggravation in his voice. "If we must go home, why don't we just go?"

She made no reply, and with a sigh of annoyance, he set off on his own.

*"MICHAEL!"*

He started violently and whirled to face her. She took his arm and led him back to the corner. "Listen darling," she said quietly. "I think ... I think there is someone..."

And then she told him. About the strange figure in the long coat. About the thick beard and wild frenzy of hair. About the way he clearly didn't want to be seen.

To her surprise though, her son didn't look even remotely afraid. In fact, he stared at her as if she was an idiot. 'That's Doctor Smelly,' he said.

'Doctor Smelly?' Kathy was baffled.

'He's a sort of tramp. He's always hanging around. Surely even you've heard of him?'

Dumbly, Kathy shook her head.

Michael rolled his eyes in disbelief. 'Honestly, where've you been? He walks around every night.'

"Who exactly is he?" From what she'd so far heard, she didn't exactly approve, but she felt a little better. Putting a name and face to the unknown was always reassuring.

"They say he used to be a doctor down at the Infirmary. You know ... a surgeon. Only, someone supposedly died while he was operating on them, and he went bonkers. He's been walking about ever since."

Almost subconsciously they'd started walking again. The more she heard about Doctor Smelly, the better Kathy felt, though it wasn't an edifying tale.

"Everyone says that he's trying to work up the courage to do another operation," Michael said. "He supposedly carries all his equipment in that briefcase with him. He's all right, though. He looks scary, but a few of us have even spoken to him. People should want to help him, not run away from him."

They reached their own drive, and Kathy stared up it. It would have helped, she realised, if she'd put the outside lights on. Darkness hung over the porch like canvas. Michael marched straight up, however, and warily she followed. She didn't dare look sideways, but could easily picture a ragged, long-haired figure standing there under the trees, a coat buttoned down to his ankles, the leaves and twigs rustling as he shuffled towards her, moonlight streaking his dank, lice-infested hair and maniacal eyes.

She reached the front door, sweating, turned the key quickly and opened up. Michael walked jauntily in. She looked back. The drive was bare of life, as she'd of course known it would be. She shook her head, closing the door and locking up behind her.

A few minutes later, they were upstairs and getting ready for bed.

Michael switched some music on, but Kathy shouted through the bedroom wall for him to turn it off; it was way too late at night! Grudgingly, she imagined, he did. Shortly afterwards, she heard him going into the bathroom, then the tap came on.

Thankfully, she stripped off and climbed into bed. The duvet, having been left rolled-back for the last twenty minutes, had aired itself nicely and was deliciously soft and warm. It didn't seem quite so frightening out there now, she reflected, switching off her bedside light and snuggling down. It was just another town at midnight. No one around, everything at peace. Kathy felt sleep stealing over her in that old luxurious way.

Next door, Michael turned over in bed, the springs creaking.

But no, that had to be wrong. Surely she could still hear him in the bathroom, washing his hands? It was a real scrub-up too, by the sound of it.

What was he trying to do, she wondered, sterilise them?

\* \* \*

\* \* \*

Paul Finch is an ex-cop and journalist turned best-selling author. He first cut his literary teeth penning episodes of the The Bill, and has written extensively in horror and fantasy, including for Dr Who.

He is best known for his crime/thriller novels, of which there are twelve to date, one of which, *Strangers*, made the Sunday Times Top 10.

His brand new historical epic, *Usurper*, was published in April 2023.

# BEST SERVED COLD

## F.D. QUINN

I dream of fondant potatoes in danger of drowning under thick meat juice. I visualise an abundance of seafood crowned with a fluffy, yet crisp topping. I imagine rivulets of crème anglais slipping down the moulded ridges of a dense chocolate mousse. This is my dream. You and Lynn, both of you have given me the chance to make it real and I'll never forget that. The windows are steamed already from the damp travellers packed into the express coach to Edinburgh. A judder to start and we are off. I am on my way to train at Chez Dubois.

The glass is cold against my flushed cheek and the vibration of the engine echoes all the way to my teeth. The woman next to me is squashed into the seat, sharing it with her bag. Even though I'm not fat there is not a lot of room. Ok, maybe my backside shows I love food. 'Never trust a skinny cook,' you declared at our meal each night. Lynn is on the skinny side. I am more ample but that's what I am, a cook, a real cook.

It's taken a hard week to complete all my food prep in

time to leave. I can relax now as through a haze of drizzle we trundle past The Avenue, with my favourite butchers and the overpriced deli, onward, past the new super-market and towards my goal. You haven't clocked how busy I've been, cooking and packing. I even squeezed in a short blunt haircut for a professional look. I've been married fifteen years to a man who doesn't see me, even when he isn't studying worthy literature. No, you haven't noticed my frantic preparations. My final engagement before leaving was Lynn's party for the book club. 'A small select intellectual group.' Wasn't that how you praised it?

Lynn called last month, 'It's about the book club dinner. Would the first Tuesday suit?'

'Oh yes.' I thought I'd wear the blue wrap dress, it skims all my curves and I can tie it loose if need be.

Her voice cut through my thoughts, 'Can you make the dessert as well?' she added. She wanted me to let her pass the food off as hers — a girl's secret, she had whis-pered. I agreed because at the time I guess I was in awe of her. 'You're so clever at this kind of thing,' she trilled. Not clever enough for a bloody invite mind, despite reading the wretched book.

I learned long ago to keep my features flat and tongue still, so that no one could read my mind. Not even you, my dear husband, knew the bitter disappointment I felt. 'It's not your kind of thing,' you said and continued reading. But I'm done with pretending. I exchange a tentative smile with my neighbour and offer her a home-made cookie. We munch in companionship as the bus smoothly edges out into the motorway traffic.

My head bumps against the window each time I lose my fight to stay awake. Exhausted but determined to miss nothing, I sit up straight, dust the crumbs from my chest and pay attention to each feature of the landscape that marks my escape. Breaking free to cook at a restaurant ranked in the top fifty eateries in Britain. You don't think I'm well read, do you darling? You're mistaken. I read cookbooks and all the restaurant reviews. The Scotsman this month reviewed Chez Dubois as serving '*dishes of serious intent with emphatic flavours.*' That's just what I aspire to, with '*the ingredients themselves doing the talking*'. Now that's real literary prose!

It's hard to believe I'm beginning a new life and you both gave me the freedom without ever knowing. Do you remember when we were decorating the dining room and I fell off the ladder? I fell on my side and the whack forced all the air out of my body and the thoughts from my brains. I forgot to breathe and didn't remember that I had to. That's what it felt like when I overheard you with Lynn and realised what a cheating weakling you really were. Did you ever love me?

From far away I watched myself get up, work, cook and stare at you eat across the table. Numb, anaesthetised, I couldn't taste a thing. Everything was dry and dusty on my tongue. Then last week I enjoyed a comfortable warm feeling like chocolate melting in my mouth. Lynn's barbecue was rained off and her unhappiness at her wet burger buns gave me a germ of an idea that began to grow.

So, I did the only thing I could. I began to cook for the book club dinner, a parting gift for you and your mistress Lynn. Maybe one day I'll share my recipes with you both. I marinated the venison in red wine and juniper berries for two days. The gin-scented mix was intoxicating. Then I sautéed the onions and pan fried the dog food, before adding stock to form a thick sauce and cooking it all together slowly at a low heat. You said last time it was moreish with the paté. I'm sure you will agree the dog food makes a fine substitute.

The fish pie is true luxury, with cod, smoked haddock, scallops and a little secret special touch, cat food. I didn't want to scrimp on ingredients, so I used a premium brand. If you want to recreate the dish, it's available from most good supermarkets. Lynn always had the look of a satisfied cat in front of a fire. Once I knew why she had that overly pleased look on her face, dear husband, I knew I had to remove it. The fish pie is inspired by her Cheshire-cat grin.

Any good literary or culinary work should have a spectacular finish. The chilled chocolate bavarois is special in every way. A dish created by the world's first celebrity chef and served to Napoleon, the Tsar and George IV. You do love chocolate, don't you darling? I prepared it in advance and know you will all enjoy Lynn's 'handmade delicacy'. How memorable it will be. For all my lack of reading, I do know that revenge is a dish best served cold. The chill masks the taste of the Verpanol, which I swirled into the chocolate and brandy at the last minute. Not a common ingredient, Verpanol, and difficult to find since its withdrawal. You remember, don't you, my love? We watched it together on Panorama – the anti-depression wonder drug shelved after they discovered the distressing, sometimes permanent, side effect of erectile dysfunction when taken with alcohol.

The rumble of the bus engine has stopped, we've arrived! Oooh, how I love the Capital. Now, I mustn't forget my brolly. It's been delicious going over this in my mind but I must leave you behind to start a new style of cooking. I do hope I get to discover what you thought of the dessert.

\* \* \*

\* \* \*

Fiona Quinn is a Glasgow child of the '70s, a science nerd and fiction lover. She has written all her life but focused on scientific articles and corporate reports as she worked across Europe, the Middle East and Africa. On returning to Scotland to live, she joined a local writing group and studied creative writing at UWS. This resulted in her being welcomed into the supportive book and writing community and a new life: going to book festivals and hanging out with amazing authors.

As a doctor of chemistry, Fiona has an unhealthy understanding of dangerous chemicals, poisons and how to dissolve bodies. Fortunately, rather than applying this knowledge to committing crime – she writes it. When her dog, husband and three children allow, she enjoys writing short stories that reflect her eclectic love of books. Her short story *'Getting Away'* was published in the 2nd Crime and Publishment Anthology. She is currently writing her second novel, a crime thriller set on the west coast of Scotland.

# A FACE FOR MURDER

## JUDITH O'REILLY

Hey everyone, thank you so much for joining me. My name is Ashley Tootles. This is 'A Face for Murder', and wow! I mean – wow! I'm really pumped about today's show.

Okay, so while I apply my latest glamour make-up look – and take note, we are heavy on the smoky eye today – I'll be telling you all about the murder of Maisie Carter. AKA – The Girl Who Ran Away. Cue the sinister music! (Sienna is wrangling the tech for me. Don't mess up, Sienna! I'm kidding – she's super smart.)

Right, to celebrate our one millionth subscriber, we decided to do something special. As you know, we're all about putting the beauty into True Crime. And usually while I apply my make up, I talk you through the details of a real life True Crime case. This time – wait for it – we went out on the road and did our own investigation into Maisie's murder! We are loco, huh!

Do you like what I'm doing with my foundation? Yep, you're right. Guilty as charged. I'm using the exact same primer as I applied on my Jack the Ripper show. But, shoot me. Or should I say – stab me! – I know for a fact this particular foundation goes on really well over it. (Quick reminder: all the products are listed at the bottom of the video.)

We chose the Maisie Carter mystery for this special treatment because I felt really upset when her body was found last month. I didn't just think 'Hooray, here's another murder mystery that my subscribers are going to love'. No! Because I'm not a monster. I'm interested in monsters, sure I am. But then, you are too, because you wouldn't be here otherwise. I am super aware of the need to be sensitive. Victims are people too. And they have families, and those families, they're nearly all of them people too. And friends. People also. I get that. Which reminds me, sometime soon, I'll be doing a 'Get Ready With Me' make-up show with products all aimed at sensitive skin. One to watch out for if you're prone to breakouts.

And I think part of my upset was her age. I mean look at that photo. Maisie was gorgeous, and not that there's a good age to be murdered, because there really isn't. But 17! That sucks big time. Talking of age, I need a truck load of concealer today, don't I? That's because it's been party central here since the conviction of Annie the Cannibal out in Sydney, Australia. Life sentence. Whoop, whoop! Am I right? I don't want to fat shame Annie, because frankly, I don't think that's a very nice thing to do to another woman, but seriously, I hope she gets some help with her appetite in prison. I don't just mean what she eats. I mean how much she eats, right!

What do you think? Is that enough concealer? No more tequila for me, it goes straight to my eyebags.

And don't worry, before we uploaded this video, we told the detective in charge of the investigation everything we found out, and she was thrilled. If you're watching this, DI Sharon Oates – you're welcome.

Let's start at the beginning. So, 21 years ago in 2001, Maisie Carter runs away from home. Or that's what everyone thinks. Her dad Frank is a farmer on the North Northumberland coast. He is super strict. Her mum Val is 10 years younger than Frank, and everyone we met up there told us what a lovely person she is. (Val is still alive, but unfortunately she has dementia now). This is a photo of the farmhouse where the Carters lived. It's pretty grim right? And it's three miles outside the nearest village, a place called Seaport.

Maisie is super talented and wants to go to art school, but the problem is – she never turns up to her first A level exam. When her art teacher rings up to find out why, Maisie's mum tells him that the night before there was a quarrel, and that Maisie got upset. Val later tells police that the minute she puts down the phone, she runs up to Maisie's bedroom, and finds revision books open on the desk but her rucksack and purse, favourite clothes, makeup and art portfolio are all missing.

Val is super upset. She rings the police to tell them Maisie has run away after a row about £200 going missing from a biscuit barrel in the kitchen. The police come up to the farmhouse to talk to Val and Frank, and to Maisie's older brother Jackie. Val says she believes her daughter left the house around quarter to one in the morning, because that's when she heard the farm collie dog bark. Eighteen-year-old Jackie, however, says he got home from Newcastle just past one, and seeing her light was still on he knocked on Maisie's door. She didn't open it, just told him to get lost. At this point, the police aren't worried, but they decide to drop by Maisie's school and talk to her girlfriends – Lauren, Emma and Fiona. Sienna, can we have the photo?

Lauren is Head Girl and editor of the school newspaper. She's the blonde in the 'Little Miss Bossy' tee shirt on the driver's side of the Mini.

Emma is the one with bad skin leaning up against the passenger door. It's actually her car. (While I think, I'm going to add a fantastic glycolic spot treatment to my product list.)

Fiona is the one with the glasses and plaid shirt by the open boot. Sidebar: she's had laser treatment now, so no spectacles. She still has the same haircut though. I don't know why.

The three friends are still really tight and initially, they didn't want to talk to us. They kept saying things like "Leave it to the police. Blah blah! What's this got to do with mascara? Duh!" Luckily for us, Lauren's eldest daughter is a fan of the show and told her mum it might help find Maisie's killer. She even dug out that photo for us!

The three friends all tell the police that Maisie didn't get on with her dad and that her brother used to beat up on her. Fiona says that Maisie couldn't wait to leave home and had regularly suggested they run away to London. Fiona advised Maisie to stick it out so she could take up her place at art college. Fiona even took out her phone and showed us a self-portrait of Maisie, which she still has hanging above her fireplace in her living room in Chelsea.

Just going to apply the blusher now. Big brush, see. Then, blend like you're a psycho trying to fit in.

We know that in the weeks following Maisie's disappearance, her family travel down to London looking for her. They put up posters and go round hostels. But no one has seen Maisie. After a year, Jackie joins the army. After three years, Lauren marries her childhood sweetheart Sam. And why wouldn't you – the guy's family own a stately home. Plus he's cute, huh?

Emma goes into the family funeral business.

And Fiona becomes a big City lawyer in London.

No one hears from Maisie – ever. Ten years ago, Frank dies after a heart attack and Maisie's mother tries to find her all over again. Contacts the Salvation Army this time. Nothing. But at least, Jackie comes back from the army and takes over the farm.

Okay, so this is where it gets interesting.

Last month, there's a huge storm over North Northumberland. Power lines are down. Roofs are off. Trees come down. Including an ancient oak tree on the Carter farm. A tree which is in a field close by a stone wall. A field way distant from the farmhouse, but pretty close to a lane which locals use as a cut-through. And when the oak tree comes down, the roots tear themselves out of the ground, and the whole thing topples over. Kerboom. The next morning, it's chaos. But when Jackie goes walkabout to assess the damage on the farm, what does he see tangled in the roots of the uprooted oak?

I'm going to apply my eyeshadow now. Don't you love

these colours. Kinda reminds me of a black eye. In a good way.

A skull.

He knows straight away. It's Maisie. When he rings the police, that's what he tells them. Let's listen to the recording we managed to get hold of. (Don't ask me how. Sienna's a wonder.)

*'I think I just found my sister's body.'*

*'Can you tell me your name and where you're calling from.'*

*'Oh my God.'*

*'Sir, can you tell me your name.'*

*'My name's Jackie Carter. We thought she'd run away.'*

He sounds shocked right. Not shocked enough for the police though. They turn up to the farm. Go out to the tree, and yes, there are skeletal remains in the ground. They re-open the investigation into Maisie's disappearance. Except now, it's a murder investigation.

Just to say, I'm not that into contouring at the moment. I think it's had its day. But I will still do a stripe here and here down either side of my nose and a highlight stripe on my nose and chin. But you have to keep it subtle, right.

Anyway, along with what's left of Maisie after 20 years, the forensic team also discover fragments of canvas and clothing, scraps of leather, as well as an old mobile phone which they go to work on. The fragments indicate that Maisie had indeed packed up her belongings, and that she was in the process of running away. Except Maisie never made it.

The police bring Jackie in for questioning. Jackie says he never beat up Maisie. He caught her with drugs one time and took them off her. When she tried to get them back, he pushed her away. He says he loved Maisie, but she was often 'a giant pain in the arse' and 'a compulsive liar'. Obviously, he denies killing her.

Meanwhile, the post-mortem comes back. Don't ask how, but we have a copy! You catch more flies with honey, Sienna always says. I have no idea what that means. But she's a machine. So, the pathologist has checked the teeth against Maisie's dental records, and confirms the body is hers. The report says that Maisie *"suffered damage to the side of her skull consistent with a single blow"* and a broken wrist which they speculate could have happened when she fell. The pathologist also points to a large stone found in the shallow grave, which has trace elements of dried blood on it. He says the injuries are consistent with the theory that the stone was the murder weapon.

Sienna and I start wondering if someone caught Maisie running away? Maybe her super strict dad? Well, Frank isn't around to ask. And Maisie's mum is away with the fairies. But Jackie said his father was convinced Maisie had run away from home, that he blamed himself, and was left a broken man by it.

We went back to talk it all through with Maisie's friends.

Lauren was a straight-A student, but had decided to take a year off before she went to uni. She gets a job in the café attached to Sam's stately home and within a few months, she's engaged to him – they're married by the time she's 21. We asked her about the drugs Jackie mentioned. Was Maisie involved with the wrong kind of people? Had she bought drugs she couldn't pay for? Was that why the money was missing from the biscuit barrel?

Lauren admits that the four girls used to smoke cannabis together regularly and had taken ecstasy a couple of times. Sam had a supplier in Newcastle, and whatever he didn't use – he sold on to friends. She says that Maisie didn't owe Sam or anyone else money, but that yes, as Jackie said, she wasn't always a nice person. For instance, her nickname for Sam was 'Dim Sam'. And she was a liar. For instance, the week she was murdered, Maisie had told lies about Emma stealing from the dead at her dad's funeral home.

Hold on. Fake eyelash emergency. Give me a second. There you go.

When we talk to Emma, she claims the other three girls were prettier, smarter and more popular. That they weren't always nice to her, but that she had a car and was useful to them. She used to come out from the village to take Maisie to school every morning, for instance. Even so, she says Maisie was a bully, and that she regularly refused to sit next to her in form, because she claimed that she smelled like dead people. Emma said she ended up spending a fortune on shower gels and perfumes. When Sienna asks about the argument, Emma says Maisie had accused her of stealing diamond earrings from a corpse, but that on the very evening she disappeared, she'd called to apologise, describing it as a 'wind-up'. Maisie had confided that she and Fiona were going out, and that the pressure of keeping the relationship a secret was getting to her.

Oh, and while I think. We have a sponsor to thank for their support today. Just Fabulous! is a monthly subscription service that for as low as £10 a month gives you access to premium beauty and skincare products at discounted prices. If I didn't already have beauty companies literally begging me to use their products, I would almost definitely probably take out a subscription to Just Fabulous! Check out their socials, guys. And use the code AFACEFORMURDER for 10% off your subscription.

At school, Fiona was already 'out' by the way. Maisie, however, wasn't. Fiona admitted that she was passionately in love with Maisie and had been for years, but Maisie didn't feel the same way. In fact, for a long time she'd suspected that Maisie was two-timing her with Sam, not least because she'd seen him give Maisie a stack of money.

So, what we have is a brother, who may or may not have been violent with his sister some time before her death.

Lauren, who had cause to be jealous, because rumour had it Maisie was sleeping with Sam.

Emma, who was bulled by Maisie and wrongly accused of being a thief.

Fiona, who loved Maisie, but who believed she was being betrayed by Maisie.

And 'Dim Sam' himself. Why was he giving Maisie money? Had she threatened to expose his drug dealing to his family or to the police? That was Sienna's theory, anyway, so we put it to him, and Sam didn't deny it. Just called the pair of us some very bad names.

We had to buy a whiteboard.

Jackie might have had the opportunity to kill his sister, but he didn't have an obvious motive.

Each of her friends however had their own reasons to kill Maisie.

What about the opportunity though?

The farm was three miles outside the village. Forensics indicated that Maisie had brought her bag outside the farmhouse. Was she waiting for a lift?

Both Sam and Emma had cars. Had Maisie persuaded one of them to pick her up and drive her to the local train station, or better yet Newcastle train station an hour away? When they arrived, did an argument blow up about the bullying, or the drugs?

Neither Lauren nor Fiona had their own cars, although Lauren sometimes borrowed Emma's car. We saw her about to drive it in the photograph of the three of them. Fiona had a bicycle but couldn't drive a car. Could she have cycled out to the farm with the intention of persuading Maisie to stay? And did tempers become heated?

We know Maisie had an exam the next day. Indeed, her revision books were open on her desk when her mother went into her room. But, as Sienna pointed out, why revise if you're going to run away?

After 20 years in the grave, it took time for the police to salvage the received text messages and the record of the calls in and the calls out. The night of her death, Emma and Maisie did indeed talk.

But Maisie didn't call Emma to apologise. I believe she called Emma to accuse her of the theft of the £200 cash from the biscuit barrel. After all, Emma had the chance to steal the money when she gave Maisie a lift to school that morning. Perhaps Emma took it – not because she was a thief – but because she wanted Maisie to know how it felt to be wrongly accused.

But Maisie wasn't so easily brought to heel. I think she accused Emma – rightly this time - and then told one of her famous lies. Perhaps that her mother Val had seen Emma steal the money? Understandably, Emma panicked.

The other call that came into Maisie's phone that night was from a number listed under 'Dim'.

Twenty years ago, Sam was quite the ladies' man. I'm guessing Emma called him in hysterics. To calm her down, he suggested they'd go talk to Maisie together. Then Emma could give her back the £200.

Somehow, he persuaded Maisie to come out to the oak tree. Maybe he told her he had drugs for her? Or more blackmail money? I don't think Sam and Emma went there with the intention of murdering Maisie. But when Maisie refused to listen to Emma's pleading...

Hold on while I line my lips. You need a steady hand.

...a panicking Emma picked up a piece of the crumbling dry-stone wall and...

Okay, where is that lipstick brush. Ah, here we go...

... smashed Maisie over the head with it.

These two aren't exactly Rose and Fred West.

So Sam reached out to the girl who always knew exactly what to do – Lauren. And, as ever, Little Miss Bossy took charge. Lauren snuck out of her own house, and drove Emma's mini over to Fiona's house. She explained the situation, and together the two of them drove to the oak tree. Just how organised was Lauren? Organised enough to pick up a couple of spades from the garden shed? I think so.

Lauren and Fiona chose to help. Lauren, because Sam would have to marry her now. But if he went to prison, her dream of a big house and a wealthy husband was over.

As for Fiona? Is it too much to believe Maisie's death came as something of a relief?

The others certainly needed Fiona on board for Lauren's plan to work. Fiona was a regular visitor to the farm. Which is why Maisie's mother paid no heed when the dog barked and then quietened as she let herself into the house. When Jackie knocked on his sister's door and was told "Get lost, Jackie", he presumed it was his sister. It was, in reality, Fiona packing up Maisie's things, because it had to look as if Maisie was running away.

I'm guessing, afterwards, the four of them made a pact. That if Maisie's body was ever found, they would point the finger at each other. Knowing as time passed, the evidence, such as it was, would never be enough to incriminate one of them on their own.

After all, it's 20 years ago and no one can prove there was ever a call between Dim Sam and Lauren that night.

And their plan would have worked, if only Fiona hadn't kept Maisie's portfolio. The rucksack of clothes and make-up, the purse, all went into the grave with Maisie. But not the portfolio. She even had Maisie's self-portrait framed, remember. After all, Maisie's art was all she had left of the girl she'd once loved. The girl she still loves perhaps? Unfortunately for Fiona, Maisie's old art teacher kept detailed records of his students' work and the contents of their portfolios. We checked with him.

I'm sure all four old friends are watching today's show, and I'm guessing Fiona will be the first to confess her part in the mystery of Maisie Carter's disappearance. I suspect she's still sad about how it went down. We'll be sure and do an update in the event of a trial. We took advice on this show from lawyers. They warned us someone might sue. Of course, it would help their case if they were innocent. If Fiona doesn't have that portfolio stashed in her attic some place. See you in court, guys.

Okay, so that's it for today. Really hope you like this date night glam look. Join us next time on 'A Face for Murder' when we'll be examining the case of Dr Crippen. And the look I'll be going for is sun-kissed Californian beach babe. See you soon, true crime nerds! Keep it criminal and keep it beautiful.

\* \* \*

*Copyright © 2023 Judith O'Reilly*

\* \* \*

Judith O'Reilly is the author of three page-turning action-adventure thrillers featuring government spy and ex-assassin, Michael North. The Financial Times described her latest thriller, *Sleep When You're Dead*, as one of the 'Best Books of 2022'. Lee Child has described her writing as 'terrific' and David Baldacci as 'a sheer delight'. O'Reilly is also the author of two memoirs including the UK and German bestseller *Wife in the North* (a BBC Radio 4 Book of the Week) and *A Year of Doing Good* (during which she tried - and failed - to become a better person). She is a former journalist with the Sunday Times, Channel 4 News and Newsnight.

# A ROUTINE EXTRACTION

## JOHN LAWRENCE

The Cedar Tavern was filling up when I heard a soft voice beside me at the bar.

"Hey. Buy you a drink?"

I looked at her in the bar mirror. I didn't know her, but that wasn't necessarily bad. I lowered my voice to match hers, still looking at the mirror. "Do you know someone I know?"

"Marcy."

"Can you tell me something to prove it?"

"I know where she lives."

If that were true, she possibly did know Marcy. Most people know only where they think she lives. "That's not much. Everyone knows the place on West 8$^{th}$..."

"Not that one. The one with the ... quiet neighbours."

So she did know Marcy. Or know someone who did. Still not enough.

I studied the young woman's reflection. She looked ground down. Didn't meet my eyes in the mirror. So far, so good.

But some angry husband could have picked up a vulnerable-looking girl and be running her. Marcy was on a quiet case, so I couldn't check.

"So, what's your story?"

"My boyfriend hits me."

&#42; &#42; &#42;

"Order a drink. For yourself." I looked directly at her for the first time.

When she had a rum and coke in front of her, I said, "Marcy didn't mention you."

When I'd turned to face her, I had scanned the crowd. Seemingly safe. Moncrieff was in his usual spot, and had raised an eyebrow, so I knew he was on the job.

The girl said, "I talked to her months ago. I didn't take her advice. Stupid."

"She mention me?"

"No."

"Then how did you find me?"

"I couldn't find Marcy, so I asked around."

Not good. Whether someone dirty was on to us, or the people who needed us had discovered our connection, it was still not good. My questions came fast now.

"Who said to look for me here?"

"Buster."

Must talk to him.

"Your name?"

"Susan Grabowski."

"Address?" She gave it, fast.

"Born where?"

"Greenpoint."

"Parents alive?"

"Yes. Lukasz and Barbara Grabowski. Still in Greenpoint!"

I was scaring her. Good.

"Boyfriend's name?"

"Steve Garcia."

"Same address as you?"

"Yes."

"Does he know your parents?"

"Yes."

"His parents' names?"

"Anthony and Natalie."

"Address?"

"Somewhere near Lincoln Center; he's never introduced me."

"They're more traditional than your parents?"

"Very."

"Exactly how and when does he hit you?"

Her eyes filled up. "With his fist. Wherever it doesn't show. If he doesn't like breakfast. After he talks to his father. If I spend too long at the grocery store. He's scared off everyone I know. The only people I'm allowed to see are my parents. They didn't raise me for this. I swear, I think he's going to kill me."

I slowed down. "Only you know the truth of that. Are you sure you want to take Marcy's advice? Do you know what it means?"

"Yes," she said, right away. Then more slowly, "I think so."

I rolled my neck as if working out the kinks. In the back of the tavern, Moncrieff finished his drink, smoothed his hair – vain bastard – said goodbye to the regulars and slouched out the door.

"OK, let's go." I slid off the bar stool as gracefully as possible, using the foot rail for support. It was a long way down.

Susan said, "I thought you'd be..."

"Bigger."

* * *

Most people who knew I was a martial artist (and there weren't a lot) thought I took it up because I was so small. To give me a fighting chance if someone tried to rape me in the subway. That was OK; it was a good cover story, and in that summer of 1974, the New York City subways were a pit.

In truth, I became a fighter because I'd always had the need to defend the undefended. Not the obvious life choice for a girl who was four foot ten and 95 pounds.

To strangers' eyes, and unless they looked directly into mine, I was a helpless, tiny thing.

I had a necessarily close relationship with my physio-therapist. When not bitching about how I undid all her good efforts, Carlotta even approved of my work.

She damn well should have. Since my intervention, Carlotta's mother was living in Portland, Oregon – trying to civilize my sister's tribe of warrior children. Under another name. Limited to contacting Carlotta by a system of mail drops. But safe.

* * *

Lots of people assumed Moncrieff was gay. He wasn't; he was just privileged and English.

That summer, when everyone wore jeans and T-shirts, he always looked as if he'd strolled off the cricket ground at Lord's. In 1925. Baggy white flannel trousers, a crisp white shirt, linen jacket and a tie that probably denoted some exclusive school. Sleek yellow hair and white buckskin shoes, for heaven's sake.

Moncrieff never sat when he could lounge. Never drank a beer when he could sip a gin and tonic. Never called anyone by name, just "old boy" or "dear thing".

You either admired his style or thought "affected" didn't go halfway far enough.

I suspected that as a kid, he'd suffered a good many knocks and bloody noses on the playing fields of wherever, but I knew that by the time he'd achieved adulthood, he was unbroken. And unchanged.

You had to know what to look for to recognize that Moncrieff's baggy whites camouflaged a lean and muscled body. And you had to know him much, much better to know that his real difference was inside:

At some point during his private education, Moncrieff had internalized the English code of fair play to an extreme degree. He couldn't stand to see an underdog stranded without a champion.

That made us natural partners.

How we met, and how we discovered our affinity, is a story for another time.

\* \* \*

While Moncrieff was researching Susan's story (the relatives all lived where Susan said they did), Carlotta gave Susan a thorough physical exam. Susan's damage was, if anything, worse than I'd expected.

I held a close interview with Buster. It turned out Susan knew someone we both trusted, so he had almost nothing to answer for. He should have asked me before mentioning my name, but I judged he wouldn't make that mistake again. It would be a bore to change my haunts and routines again, and good scouts are hard to come by. Plus we'd keep him out of the loop for a while.

A few days later, Susan and I arrived separately at Marcy's real home.

No risk in that; Susan had already been down this part of the path. And no one had seen us together; we entered from different routes through the cemetery, mine unknown to anyone except the people who needed to know.

"OK. This can go two ways. We can help you move to another borough, change your job, even change your name and get you a new driver's license. We can hide you while we're getting this done. Stop me if you've heard this before."

"No, go ahead."

"Once you walk away from Steve, you can't ever go back. To the neighborhood. To your friends' houses, to your old place of work, to your parents'. Everyone will have to come to you, and even then, they'll have to make sure they aren't followed. We can teach you how to do that. Does that sound like too much trouble to put your friends and family through?"

"No." This time, she looked straight into my eyes. "It doesn't sound like enough."

So she had been paying attention to Marcy after all.

"You're sure you need to go the other way?"

"Yes."

I stood up. "All right, then. It's the nuclear option."

* * *

It was a routine extraction.

Susan's boyfriend Steve was big and buff with dull eyes. He and another guy were drinking beer when we entered the apartment. Good. Even drunk, most guys won't attack a small woman in front of their friends; it's embarrassing. I didn't make eye contact.

Steve stood up and took a muscle-bulging stance. Not so good.

"Who the fuck are you?" He tried to square up to me, but I stepped back and to one side, so he had to square up to me again.

"Hey. Just a friend who's driving Susan to Greenpoint."

Susan chimed in, "I'm going to Mom and Dad's for the weekend, angel. You remember; I told you?"

Damn it. She sounded nervous. Something crazy lit up Steve's eyes.

"You some lezbo trying to get into my girl's pants? She never needed a driver to get to Brooklyn before." Now he came toward me, and I kept sliding just slightly to the side while looking like I was backing up in fear. He was too dumb to realize he wasn't getting a lock on me.

Susan remembered the script and picked up an overnight bag standing ready by the door. It contained all her money and some photographs the police would call evidence.

Steve's attention swiveled back to Susan. "Don't you fucking move!" But by this time, he had to turn to get to her. She was already out the door.

He tried to follow, but I'd planted my foot in front of his leading leg and he sprawled over it, landing face-first. I risked a quick look at his friend, but the guy was just sitting there with a "not my fight" look on his face. So Steve's friends didn't give a shit about him, either. Good to know.

I was hoping to be out the door without any more unpleasantness, but the idiot was on his feet and took a run at me. I settled my weight as his Adam's apple ran into the heel of my right hand; lifting him off his feet as he retched and then collapsed. This time I got out.

I slammed down the stairs, flew through the front door and around the corner. Moncrieff and Susan were in the van, engine running. A moment later we were heading for the West Side Highway and possible safety for Susan.

Big breath in, a longer breath out.

"OK. Tell me what you're going to do."

"Take the bus to Schenectady. Someone named Margy will meet me. She'll put me on another bus and tell me what to do next."

"And if anything goes wrong?"

"I call the number I memorized."

"Repeat it." She did.

"And what can you never do?"

Silence.

"Susan."

"Never contact my parents. Never contact anyone I know. Never..." She stopped.

"I know ... I know. Sooner or later, we'll let you know how and when you can write to your parents. But you have to accept you may never see them again. It's too soon to tell. We'll keep tabs on Steve, but no promises. Will you do this?"

"Yes."

And maybe she would.

\* \* \*

I didn't understand why I was so tired. Everything had gone as planned. Moncrieff returned from the Port Authority relaxed; no one had followed them – not that we'd expected it – and Susan was on the bus.

Was the extreme solution the right solution? I had no way of knowing. Susan thought she was going to be killed; I believed her. Maybe Steve was one of those obsessive guys who would try to track her down through her friends and family. Or maybe five years from now he'd be fat and happy with a submissive wife and three frightened children. And even then, if he caught wind of her, he might try and track her down anyway.

For the moment, it was out of my hands.

"What's up, pussycat?" said Moncrieff. A slick legend in his own mind.

"I'm nobody's kitten, dickwad." But I returned his goofy grin.

He touched my shoulder lightly. "Spot of mindless physical comfort, old thing?"

When I woke in the morning, he was still holding my hand.

\* \* \*

*Copyright © 2023 John Laurence*

\* \* \*

John Laurence wasted his youth working in New York, Boston, San Antonio, San Francisco, Tokyo and London. Now settled in Cambridge, England, he devotes himself to writing and behaving disgracefully with writers-and-readers cabal The Old Peculiars.

# A SLICE OF LIFE

MIK BROWN

**His Story**

A marriage simply doesn't break down overnight. It's a gradual process. Like the melting of the glaciers. Bit by bit, piece by piece, unnoticed at first. The things we once found cute now grind away at our patience before exploding in a spectacular supernova of a fight. There were countless emotional waves eroding the coastline right under our noses and we don't see them until they've broken away enough of the foundations that held us together. Word by hurtful word, each stubborn silence growing longer. It's only when we look back, when they're stitched together like a series of time-lapse stills in an Attenborough documentary, that you curse yourself for not stopping the decay in time to do anything about it.

Last night's argument was just the latest in a sequence stretching back years, never truly concluded. The gaps between range from weeks to months, but there is never a white flag waved. Emotions locked away while we gather strength for the next round of hostilities. Me

195

accusing her of caring more about work than starting a family. Her accusing me of not supporting her career, and the business that puts this fine roof over our heads. It's no way to live, but it's the only way we know. And it works, in a fashion. No matter how caustic the words we spew at each other, I can't imagine a world in which she isn't part of my life. Part of me. I need her.

I hear a muted orchestra of domestic sounds, kettle boiling, cutlery chiming against crockery. I want to go to her, slide my arms around her waist as she stands at the sink, push my face into her neck and inhale her scent. Whisper an apology, but pride pins me under the duvet until long after the sound of her car engine has faded. I trudge downstairs like Neanderthal man, every step weighed down by last night's whisky, until the smell of it hits me. I sniff my way into the kitchen to confirm my suspicions and sure enough, there it is perched on a wire cooling rack. A freshly baked loaf of bread. But this isn't just a loaf of bread, it's a peace offering, a time machine transporting me back to happier days. Back to the early part of the relationship. The so-called *honeymoon period*. Lazy weekends in her cosy flat overlooking the North Sea, every square inch of it regularly laced with that *fresh-from-the-oven* scent that made my mouth water like Pavlov's dog.

It's a sign of the times that over the last few years, such fits of intense baking have been reserved for apologies only. Her way of saying sorry without having to physically utter the words. I'm not judging. I do the same but with flowers or chocolates like the cliché that I am. We exchange these tokens of peace and settle back into a routine until our collective ill will reaches a critical mass again like a domestic Groundhog Day.

My stomach growls. My head thuds – a dull rhythmic bass, and I wish I could undo the previous night's decision to crack open the single malt. An internal civil war rages; my brain telling me to carve off a crust and smother it in butter. My stomach counsels caution and does a quick flip to emphasise the warning, telling all food to enter at its peril. I gently place my hand on the still-warm loaf, close my eyes, inhale deeply, consuming the scent if not the substance.

I need to clear my head first. I look longingly one last time at it, in all its enticing pale brown crusty glory and shuffle back upstairs. The hangover like a ball and chain. Ten minutes later I brave the day, recoiling in vampire-like fashion from the bright light as I open the door, looking down at my feet as I walk to save squinting into the sun. The bitter wind tugs at my hair, sliding its icy fingers down my collar as I head down Mast Lane towards the coast. Bunched fists in pockets burrowing for warmth. A faint crackle matches the rhythm of my step, the tinfoil parcel in my pocket bumping against my hand with each step. It's still warm to the touch, like a stone left out in the sun, and my fingers uncurl with a mind of their own to huddle around it.

I reach Cullercoats Bay, cross the road and pause for a moment. My head doing a full one-eighty from left to right. It never fails to impress, not even in my shabby state. The twin stone piers encircle the bay like protective arms, then off to my right the sweeping expanse of sand that is Tynemouth Longsands Beach. Even with the breeze leaching a good five degrees away from the air temperature, the beach is still speckled with figures, like a coastal version of a Lowry painting. I pick up my pace, sea air flooding my lungs, washing away my hangover one breath at a time, and before I know it I can see the boating lake on my right.

The first bench I come to has a mum and two toddlers perched on it, all three of them sucking hungrily at cartons of juice. Beyond them an old lady rises slowly from the next bench. I fancy I can hear her joints creaking from here, like a door in a haunted house, and I slide into the vacated spot before anyone else can stake a claim. She reminds me of my Nan, the way she ambles along, trailing her tartan shopping trolley behind her.

It's still early but already there's an armada of tiny boats patrolling the lake. Most of them are steered by fathers, reluctant to surrender control to sons who stand petulant, being denied the right to play with their own toys while Dad has all the fun. The briefest flicker of longing rises in me, watching other men take for granted the family I crave. It sinks again as fast as it surfaced, and I blink away a single tear that I try and chalk up to the cold air stinging my eyes, but who am I kidding?

Echoes of the night before ring in my ears, but I'm still too delicate to dwell on what the consequences will be if we don't break the impasse soon. That's a problem for this evening, tomorrow, any time but now. I just want this moment to myself, unencumbered by the obvious *what ifs*. I lean back, hands resting on my stomach, and feel the almost forgotten lump in my pocket. I'm fairly sure I could stomach it now without sacrilegious risk of bringing it back up, but when I open it I curse myself. In my haste to head out I've forgotten the damn butter.

I stand to go home and rectify the situation, tucking the bread back into the tinfoil as I do. The noise is more seductive than any Pied Piper to the resident population of ducks, and they home in on its source, like moths to a flame. Within ten seconds I have a flash mob at my feet, watching, waiting. The chorus of quacks telling me they want feeding. I look from them, to the tinfoil, and back again. I'm just about to stuff it back in my pocket and beat a hasty retreat when I see the mum on the next bench over, tapping her kids and pointing out the expectant ducks, who have now been joined by a pair of moorhens.

I can't bring myself to be *that guy* who is so tight he won't even spare a few crumbs for the birds. I begrudgingly re-open my precious parcel. To give the smaller ones a fighting chance I tear the first slice into a dozen pieces, scattering them all onto the path to my left. I repeat the process with the other slice, a crust so thick that it could probably knock a duck out cold if I launched it in one piece.

The ducks explode into action, nought to sixty faster than a sports car, and every crumb is gone in ten frantic seconds. The poor moorhens stand stunned and hungry, unable to fight their way past the tidal wave of ducks that pours over the path, scouring it clean. I look over to my right. Both kids have dissolved into laughter, and suddenly my sacrificed slices don't seem too much of a loss after all. The mum and I exchange one of those *aren't kids cute* smiles, and I decide to complete a lap of the lake before I head back home. An optimistic trio of ducks follow me for the first twenty feet, until they realise there's no more coming their way and head back into the lake, presumably to swim off the calories they've just devoured.

I take my time watching the boats again as I saunter round a lazy circuit of the water. One brave landlubber has even hired a Pedalo to impress his girlfriend, but she looks far from impressed as he goes round in slow looping circles, face red like a beetroot with the effort. I nearly take a detour into the Surf Café for a latte, but my stomach growls in dissent, and I head for home.

There's no car in the driveway when I get back. I check my phone. Nothing. I decide to have a quick cuppa and a bite to eat before I call her. I have no idea what I'll say yet, but it's always me that makes the first move. I've tried waiting her out before, but her stubbornness is of an Olympic standard. Coming in from the cold is like walking into a sauna, the damp clothes on the piping hot radiators giving a humidity level the Costa del Sol would be envious of. A cool film of sweat decorates my forehead as I move through the kitchen on autopilot.

Teabag in cup. Kettle on. Bread sliced. Butter and jam generously applied. Radio on, Gary Barlow trying to reassure me that today could be the greatest day of our lives. I beg to differ, Gary, but I've had worse. The song fades out and a bored voice rattles through the news headlines as I settle at the kitchen table. I blow ripples across the surface of a cup of tea strong enough to let the spoon stand up unaided as I listen to Rishi Sunak's bumbling attempts to fend off yet more criticism. I pull my plate closer and carve up my reward into four equal pieces. Chances are there'll be a few more slices that meet the same fate before I'm done.

*And in local news...*

I grab the piece closest to me between thumb and forefinger and wrap my mouth around a little over half closing my eyes with satisfaction. I stop mid-chew. Half turn. Listen. Listen in horror—

*Police looking for a man, twelve ducks dead, and four more fighting for their lives ... Tyneside boating lake.*

What the hell? I look at my plate as pieces fall into place.

*Police would like to speak to a man who left the scene not long after feeding them.*

The large off-white spit-ball of bread flies through the air and splats against the floor like a slushy snowball flecked with red. I hurl myself towards the sink and let the water flow into my mouth, making no attempt to swallow.

*What did she...? How could she...? She couldn't ... could she?*

I stand there, looking from the remaining three pieces of bread, to their fallen comrade on the floor, and back again. I tell myself it's a coincidence. An accident. But I can't convince myself of any alternate theory. I should call the police. No, don't be stupid. I have no proof she baked the loaf. I was the one seen feeding the ducks. They'd look at me, not her. Our marriage has survived many things, but this? If I'm right, our marriage wasn't meant to survive this, and neither was I. A permanent solution to a temporary problem.

What to do now though? Smile and make small talk when she comes home? I'm not sure that I could. There is still a small part of me that whispers, telling me I could be wrong, to give her the benefit of the doubt. How do I do that though? I might be wrong. I want to be wrong so badly. If I'm wrong, then no harm no foul. If I'm right though, do I really wait around for her to try something else? And then it hits me, and I smile a sad smile.

\* \* \*

**Her Story**

It's dark by the time I get back. His car is gone. Did it even work if he's not home? I turn on the living room light, and pause to listen. Nothing. I move through into the kitchen, heartbeat like a bass drum crashing in my ears as I flick the light switch. I'm not sure what to expect. Him lying on the floor, a chalk man drawn around him? I look in. A plate sits in the centre of the table, two slices of bread lying on it with a post-it note propped against them, its base wedged against a single red rose. I slide my glasses out of my pocket and perch them on my nose.

*Hi Emma*

*Sorry about last night. They only had one rose left but better than no flowers at all. Gone to mums for a couple of nights to give you some space. Hope you don't mind but I used most of the bread for sandwiches for the journey. Dinner's in the oven.*

*Love you*

*David*

Sandwiches for the journey? With a bit of luck, he'd eat them while driving and they'd be none the wiser, assume it was just a regular car crash. I open the oven door and peer in. He's done me one last good turn. I pull the dish towards me and grab a fork. It's been a long day and at this point I'm not fussy. I can't even be bothered to heat it up. Tuna pasta bake is the only dish he's ever perfected, but it is one of my personal favourites, especially with the generous helping of the crispy crumbed layer bubbling away on top.

\* \* \*

*Copyright © 2023 Mik Brown*

\* \* \*

Mik Brown lives in Newcastle. He is a Project Manager by day but an avid reader and writer by night. When he is not reviewing crime and thriller books he is working on his debut novel – a police procedural set in Newcastle. Mik is a regular at all the major Crime Writing and Thriller festivals so please say hi!

# VENGEANCE IS MINE

### MARK ELLIS

**London 1941**

**Tuesday, April 15th**

Frank Merlin stood in the study of a Victorian terraced house in East Putney. Before him at a large walnut desk sat the slumped corpse of successful author Magnus Charlton. There was a vivid bloodstain on the white carpet below. In the middle of the stain lay a silver letter opener, the presumed murder weapon. He became aware of a buzzing noise.

"Is that the radio I can hear?" he asked Sergeant Wilcox, the senior of the local bobbies at the murder scene.

"Yes, sir. It was blaring away when we arrived. We turned it down."

"You used gloves?"

The Sergeant bristled. "Of course, sir. We're not stupid out here in Putney, you know."

"Sorry. No slight intended. Perhaps it had been turned up to cover screams?"

"Not sure there'd have been much time for screaming. Cutting job looks very professional to me."

"You think the victim was caught unawares?"

"Seems likely. Author head down working hard at his manuscript, then ... whoosh, knife cuts throat."

"The body's exactly as you found it?"

Wilcox bristled again. "Of course, sir. Know better than to touch the body before forensics get here."

"They're on their way?"

"Supposedly. With..." An aeroplane engine droned loudly above and drowned out his voice. The officers waited with bated breath for the bomber to pass, then the Sergeant resumed. "With Jerry so busy tonight, they might struggle getting through the roads from the Yard. You had no problems, sir?"

"Came from the west. Not much happening there tonight." Merlin had been at Heston airport interviewing a pilot whose wife had gone missing. Then he'd made the mistake of calling into the office and learned that the Assistant Commissioner wanted to speak to him. He'd rung the AC at home and been told about the murder. Charlton had apparently been a friend of AC Gatehouse's wife and the AC wanted his best man on the job.

Bending down over the corpse, Merlin said, " I don't suppose it will do any harm if we move him just a touch."

Merlin gloved up and moved Charlton's shoulders so he could take a better look at the notebook beneath the dead author's head. The words 'death' and 'killer' peeked out from beneath the blood spatter.

Two forensic officers arrived, quickly followed by a police doctor. They set to work and Merlin and Wilcox adjourned to the kitchen. Charlton's house was at the end of a terrace in a cul-de-sac only a few yards from the Thames, although it had no river view. The house was comfortable but not as grand as one Merlin would have expected a bestselling author to inhabit.

"He lived on his own?" Merlin asked Wilcox.

"Yes, sir. Married, but Mr Saunders next door said he and his wife separated six months ago."

"Any idea where the wife is?"

"Not yet."

Merlin looked at his watch. It was coming up to eleven-thirty. "Where's the delivery man you say discovered the body?"

"With one of my officers outside."

"Tell me his story again."

"He arrived with a parcel and found the front door open. Shouted out but there was no answer. He was about to leave the package inside the door when he heard voices. He followed the sound of the voices upstairs and into Charlton's study where he found ... well, you know what he found."

"The voices were on the wireless?"

"Yes."

"What then?"

"He ran back down the stairs in shock. When he was calm enough to think he went next door, told Saunders what had happened, then asked to use his phone. We responded immediately."

* * *

**Wednesday, April 16th**

Merlin went straight from his Chelsea flat to Putney

the following day and spent a busy morning gathering information. He arrived back at his office just after one and sat down immediately at his desk to make notes. He'd just finished when he was joined by his Sergeant, Sam Bridges, who'd spent the morning giving evidence in a robbery trial at the Old Bailey.

"We have a new case, Sergeant. Writer, name of Charlton. Had his throat cut at his home last night." Merlin pushed his notebook across the desk. "Here."

Bridges sat down to read.

'Murder Tuesday April 15th.

Victim - Magnus Charlton, aged 40. Author of mystery novels.

Cause of death - throat cut. Left Carotid artery severed. Full pathologist report due today.

Murder weapon - silver letter opener found under desk.

Location of murder - 32 Alma Terrace Putney.

Discovery of body - Found by Arnold Frost, 30, Harrods delivery man at approximately nine thirty-five pm.

Item being delivered - leather footstool.

Marital status - married but separated from Irish wife Margaret since October 1940. Wife's current whereabouts unknown.

Children - none.

Other close relatives - brother Trevor/also his literary agent.

Publisher - Paul Harvey of Harvey Books, Covent Garden.

Details of Crime Scene - Charlton found slumped, throat slit, over desk at which he was working on a new murder story. There was a radio playing loudly in the room when the body was discovered. The front door was open when the delivery man arrived. All other windows, external doors were locked with the exception of a skylight in one of the bedrooms. On initial review, Charlton's domestic did not think anything had been stolen but this is obviously not definitive.

Witness sightings - none.

Initial potential suspect list - disturbed burglar, wife, delivery man, other.

Next steps...?'

"Not much in the way of clues then," said Bridges when he'd finished reading.

"We have the murder weapon at least. So what's your first take on the culprit? Unknown intruder or person known to the victim?"

"You say the front door was found open?"

"More likely the point of exit than entry I'd say."

"Is the open skylight a feasible point of entry?"

"A doddle for an experienced criminal. Next door has a shed to climb up on and then there are some pretty solid pipes leading to the roof. No one heard or saw anything but that's no surprise if we are dealing with a professional."

"But nothing was taken."

"So says the cleaning lady. Of course, there may have been valuables secreted away of which she knows nothing. Then again it may be that nothing is missing because Charlton discovered the burglar in the act before he'd taken anything."

Bridges shook his head. "I can't really see that. Your average burglar when caught would just scarper as quick as he could. If his way was barred he'd use fists or a blunt implement. Maybe if he was a real hard case, a revolver. But sitting a man down then cutting his throat? No. That seems ... far too personal."

"I agree." Merlin stroked his chin. "Something domestic then. Or..."

"A money dispute? A business or professional disagreement?"

"Writing doesn't strike me as the sort of profession that would give rise to violence. Hard to think of Agatha Christie creeping into a room and slitting a competitor's throat."

"Poison's more her sort of thing, sir."

"An Agatha Christie reader, eh Sergeant? You surprise me."

"The missus loves her. Brings loads of Poirots and the like back from the library. I occasionally dip in. Rubbish on policing but the stories can be all right." Bridges tugged on an earlobe. "But going back to Charlton's business, it's publishing isn't it, not just people who write? Remember last year when a publisher attacked another in court with a hammer? Violence can arise in any business."

"You're right. So let's make a start with this fellow Harvey."

Paul Harvey agreed to see them at four. He was a young man with a large mole on the right cheek of an otherwise handsome face. As they sat down, he explained that his father, the founder of the firm, had suffered a nervous breakdown a year before, and as the only son he'd felt obligated to give up his City job and take on the business. News of Magnus Charlton's death clearly shook him deeply. When he was finally able to speak, he said, "What a terrible pity. Magnus was about to move to another level. We have several other excellent names on our list but Magnus was going to supersede them all. Of course, I knew the poor chap was unwell but I had no idea things were this bad."

"He didn't die of an illness, sir" said Bridges. "He was murdered."

"Good God! How? By whom?"

Merlin filled in the bare details before asking, "Might I ask what illness Mr Charlton was suffering from?"

Harvey sighed. "I don't know. Said he was having treatment for something unspecified and gave that as a reason for seeking an extension to a book deadline. He was taking a course of powerful pills but all would soon be well."

"You had no ... um ... business difficulties with Mr Charlton?"

"No, Chief Inspector. Authors and publishers obviously have occasional disagreements about royalties and the like, but in Magnus' case we'd only just agreed to bump up his take and he seemed very happy."

"His brother was his agent, I believe?"

"Yes, but I haven't seen Trevor for a while. I negotiated this latest royalty agreement directly with Magnus. He told me Trevor had other things on his plate without being specific."

"Ever meet Mrs Charlton, sir?" asked Bridges.

"Yes. Margaret. Handsome woman. A few years

younger than him. Sadly, Magnus told me they'd separated."

"Did he explain the circumstances of the separation, sir?"

"No."

"You don't happen to know where Mrs Charlton is now?

"No again, Sergeant. Perhaps she went back to Ireland?"

Merlin thought for a moment then asked, "Did Mr Charlton keep any bad company that you know of?"

Harvey looked puzzled. "What exactly do you mean by bad company?"

"Villains, sir. I understand he wrote about them. Wondered if he knew any."

Harvey pondered. "Why yes, actually. We were having a drink not so long ago and he was talking about how he started writing. Said he'd done some mixing with what he called 'the criminal classes' for research purposes, though he admitted that he'd also got tangled up with one of them, a loan shark, when he was hard up."

"He managed to escape this fellow's clutches?"

"Didn't say but I presume so."

"He said he did this research when he started writing. When was that exactly?"

"I'd guess around '32 and '33. His first book was published in 1934."

"He mentioned no names, sir?"

"No, Sergeant. He did say he did much of this research with a friend called Willie Armstrong, another mystery writer. Very talented also. Unfortunately, Willie died in a car accident last year."

After a few more questions Merlin decided to wrap things up but he remembered to ask for the name of Charlton's doctor before they left.

"He's based in Harley Street but I haven't a name. You might have a word with my secretary on your way out. Last time he was here, Magnus asked her to arrange a taxi when he was off to see him. She should have the address at least."

\* \* \*

They returned to the Yard via Harley Street where they found Charlton's doctor and learned to their surprise that Charlton had been terminally ill with prostate cancer. Back at the office, they found Detective Constable Claire Robinson hovering at Merlin's door.

"Heard about the new case, sir. Anything I can do?"

Robinson was a recent recruit to Merlin's team. Merlin had initially been unhappy with her transfer, as she was the AC's niece and he'd worried whether the decision had been made on merit, but she had quickly justified her appointment.

"You're a keen reader aren't you, Constable?"

"Nothing better than a good book, sir."

"Read any by our victim Magnus Charlton?"

"Quite a few, sir. Mostly his earlier ones."

"Recall anything about his villains?"

"I remember there were plenty of underworld figures."

"Any loan sharks?"

She considered for a moment. "Probably, but I'm not quite sure. I've still got the books. I can check. Why, sir?"

Merlin explained what they had been told and added, "He apparently used to do this research with another writer called Willie Armstrong."

"Read him too, sir. Very good."

Merlin smiled. "I think it would help if you could go home, look through your Charlton books as quickly as you can and make a descriptive list of the main underworld characters. Then we can see if they resemble any crooks the Sergeant and I know."

"Right away, sir."

As Robinson hurried off, the telephone rang. Bridges' conversation was a brief one. There was news. "Forensics say they've found a clear set of prints on the knife, sir, and they're not Charlton's."

"That's good. And where exactly are we on print-taking?"

"Not sure. I'll call Putney."

"Make sure they print anyone remotely associated."

"The wife as well if we find her?"

"The wife as well." Merlin glanced up at the office clock. "And shouldn't we have heard from the pathologist by now?"

\* \* \*

**Thursday, April 17th**

There had been no answer at the mortuary on Wednesday evening, but Bridges got through first thing in the morning. The pathologist was a dour Ulsterman. "Which cadaver? Oh yes, the writer chap. Let me look at my notes." There was a long pause. Eventually, the man came back. "Nothing unusual. For a fellow who's had his throat cut that is. There is one thing. We found something in his stomach. Some type of powder. It's being analysed now. Expect we'll call you by lunchtime with details but don't chase us."

Bridges sighed as he put the phone down. The powder was most likely some cancer medicine, which was not much help. Bridges told Merlin the news when he arrived a moment later.

Merlin nodded. "I have news too. Better news. Wilcox called me at home this morning. The wife and brother both turned up together at Charlton's house at the crack of dawn."

"Did they know of Charlton's death?"

"They say not. I suppose they didn't see yesterday's late editions."

"Why were they there?"

"They said that last week Charlton had promised his brother some money that was owing and his wife some knick-knacks from the house. Charlton's phone line has been down since Tuesday's Luftwaffe raid so they say they took a chance on spec. Arrived early, as Charlton always started work at eight and hated being interrupted. Wilcox took them back to Putney Police Station and arranged a car. They should be here any minute."

Robinson appeared at the door. "I've got that villain list, Chief Inspector."

"Well done, Constable, we'll go through it with you now, but when the Charltons arrive, Sam, I'll let you go down and have first bite at them."

* * *

When they reconvened in Merlin's office two hours later, Bridges went first. His interview with the Charltons had unfortunately been cut short, but he had learned the significant fact that the Charlton separation was due to Mrs Charlton leaving Magnus for his brother. The new couple had rented a cottage together on Ham Common near Richmond and had lived there together since the split. They had been there all night the Tuesday of the murder but weren't sure if anyone else would be able to confirm their alibi. As Bridges had tried to push on and cover more ground, Mrs Charlton had become anxious and explained that she had an urgent hospital appointment to attend at noon. When Bridges initially agreed she could leave but on her own, she had become hysterical. Eventually, the Sergeant felt obliged to allow Trevor to go too, on the understanding they'd return to the Yard the following morning.

"You took their prints before they went?"

"Yes, sir and dropped them off at forensics myself."

"The couple didn't object?"

"No."

Discussion now turned to Robinson's list. Merlin thought he recognised four of Carlton's characters, two of whom were dead. That left Flash Harry Powell, a crook of all trades south of the river. The other was Eddie Bamber, a more heavyweight figure who featured in various gang activities and ran a loan book on the side. Both men were known to be extremely ruthless.

Robinson was sent off to make enquiries as to the likely whereabouts of these two men. An hour later they received the return call from the pathologist who reported that the substance in the stomach was a barbiturate. "Not a lethal dose I think but there was quite a lot of it."

"That's odd isn't it, sir?" observed Bridges when the call was over. "Taking a bunch of sleeping pills when you're going to work at your desk."

Robinson burst in before Merlin had a chance to reply. "Powell's behind bars in the Scrubs but Bamber's at large. I've got his last-known. It's in Battersea. I've written it down for you, sir." She held out a piece of paper. "Good work, Constable." He thought for a moment. "Best the Sergeant and I head off there straightaway. I'd be grateful if you'd man the fort."

Robinson nodded, trying hard to hide her disappointment.

Soon after Merlin and Bridges had left, the telephone rang again. She set down the book she had been reading intently and picked up the receiver to hear an excited forensics man shout down the phone "We've got a match!"

"Who is it?"

To Robinson's irritation, the officer insisted he would only give the details to Merlin.

"We missed him," were Merlin's first words to Robinson as he came through the door in the late afternoon.

Bamber's landlady had told them he'd cleared out of his room the day before, owing her three months' rent. She'd barely seen him for weeks and had little useful information to impart, and neither did the other lodgers they spoke to. The landlady's son, however, did tell them the name of a gambling joint Bamber frequented when he was flush.

Robinson gave the officers the news from forensics, which perked them up. Merlin made the return call himself. When he replaced the receiver he reported "Surprise, surprise. It's the brother."

Trevor Charlton was easy to find. He was still at his partner's side at St Thomas' Hospital. Thus there was not a long wait until Merlin and Bridges were facing the man across the table of Interview Room Three, one floor below Merlin's office. Magnus Charlton's younger brother was dark with chiselled clean-cut looks. It didn't surprise Merlin that Mrs Charlton's head had been turned. He vehemently denied killing his brother despite the fingerprint evidence. He revealed for the first time that there had been a terrible row when his brother had learned his wife was leaving him, and that Magnus' anger had been primarily directed at him, with all sorts of unpleasant threats made. This had naturally upset Trevor but was no reason for killing his brother. Whatever the prints indicated, Trevor had his alibi and relied on it. Fifty minutes into the interview, Trevor's position strengthened considerably when a call was put through to the room. Bridges took it and was told by Sergeant Wilcox that a credible near neighbour in Ham had come forward to back up the alibi. He'd been walking his dog past the Charltons' cottage and had clearly seen Trevor closing a blackout curtain at around nine fifteen. Given the police doctor's estimated time of death for Magnus, between eight and ten pm, the alibi was almost unimpeachable.

On receipt of this news, Merlin felt they needed to

take a break. Back in the office, Robinson was still manning the fort. Merlin explained the situation.

Bridges walked to the window then back. "If you allow for a little flexibility on the time of death, there was still time for Trevor to get from Ham to Putney and back and kill his brother."

"It's very tight, Sam. And I have to admit I'm still struggling to understand what motive he might have had to so viciously kill his brother."

"But what can explain the fingerprints, sir? If he touched the thing before that night, you'd think he'd remember, particularly as it's so much in his interest to do so."

Robinson cleared her throat loudly.

"You've something to add, Constable?"

"Yes, sir. I think I may have an idea as to what happened."

"You do?" Merlin was unable to suppress a tone of surprise.

"You mentioned that Charlton had a writer friend called Armstrong."

"You've read him too, you said."

"Yes. Well, going through the Charlton books made me think of Armstrong's and something began to stir in my memory. I decided to bring my Armstrong collection in today along with the Charlton books and after completing the task you gave me, I started reading the Armstrong short stories while you were out. Eventually, I found what I was looking for."

\* \* \*

**Friday, April 18th**

"Morning, Frank. I understand congratulations are in order."

The AC's lanky, desiccated figure loomed at the other side of the desk.

"We had a result on the Charlton case, yes, sir."

"I gather my niece was of some help?"

"She was indeed."

"Come on then, man. Tell me all."

"Charlton's wife took up with his brother and left him six months ago. Charlton blamed his brother entirely and determined on vengeance. Just after Christmas, he found he only had a short time to live. He formulated a plan for which he needed the help of a villain. Early in his career, he'd spent time among London's criminals researching his books. A friend, another mystery writer called Armstrong, joined him in these adventures. Charlton got to know a crook called Eddie Bamber. He knew Bamber would do anything for money. He re-established contact and explained his plan to him. Bamber jumped at it.

Charlton issued two invitations for Tuesday night this week. One to his brother and one to Bamber. Bamber knew what the invitation was about. Trevor Charlton did not. All Trevor knew was that the visit would supposedly be to his advantage. Bamber was to arrive around eight thirty, Trevor at nine thirty. I should mention that on a previous visit, Magnus had got his brother drunk and placed the letter opener in his hands to get his finger-prints on it.

On the night, at some point before his first guest arrived, Charlton took sleeping pills to make himself oblivious to everything. Bamber arrived on time, climbing through an open skylight and entered the house. He found Charlton slumped at his desk, picked up the letter opener with gloved hand, and slit his throat. Then he made his escape through the front door. We managed to track him down last night to a club where he was drunkenly splashing wads of cash around. We were in luck and he soon admitted to everything."

"Did we know the brother was at the scene of the crime?"

"He never was. This part of the story, by the way, about the brother's invitation, only came out when he realised he was in the clear. Trevor was about to leave for Putney on Tuesday night when he found his car wouldn't start. He rang his brother to cry off but the phone lines were down thanks to the Luftwaffe. Even if they'd been open, of course, no one would have answered as by then Charlton was drugged or dead."

"So that saved him?"

"No. The confirmed alibi was his salvation. If not for that, the fingerprints alone might well have done for him. Getting Trevor to the house was just belt and braces for Magnus."

The AC sat back, smiling. "How on earth did you work all this out?"

"DC Robinson found the same plot in one of Willie Armstrong's short stories. 'Vengeance Is Mine' it's called. Magnus decided to take a leaf out of his friend's book, so to speak. Thank goodness for DCI Robinson's reading habit."

The AC beamed one of his gummy smiles. "I was always the one encouraging Claire to read."

"Then it seems it is I who owe congratulations to you, sir!"

\* \* \*

\* \* \*

Mark Ellis is a thriller writer from Swansea and a former barrister and entrepreneur.

He is the creator of DCI Frank Merlin, an Anglo-Spanish police detective operating in World War II London. His books treat the reader to a vivid portrait of London during the war, skilfully blended with gripping plots, political intrigue and a charismatic protagonist.

Mark Ellis is a member of the Crime Writers Association and his third book was longlisted for the CWA Historical Dagger in 2018.

Visit www.markellisauthor.com

# IT TAKES THREE DROPS

## G.L. WARING

She sees blood-red rivers against her eyelids as the burning morning sun touches her face. Her head turns as she hides from the day, grasping at the edge of a dream. In it she saw her dad, his face glowing with pride that she had been selected to join the immunisation and vaccination programme. His whole life he had worked to eradicate disease, rising through the ranks of the World Health Organisation to his current elevation. She, his little shadow, followed him into the field to battle this insidious disease. She has better tools now to do what he could not. Hard as she tries, he dissipates and she makes out the vague shape of a lab-coated figure moving quietly, trying not to awaken her. They know she will have a gruelling day ahead, so allow her the maximum respite she can get. At least that would be true if it was Miriam in the Lab, but she knows it is not.

It is him.

He is trying to move silently, not out of concern for an

overworked and zealous colleague, but to mask his indus-try. He has made no real attempt to get to know the women at the field hospital. He assumes he is in charge while the Doctor is out in the field. He makes no effort to speak any language other than his own, and a strangled approximation of what he informs them is French. He has never been to the Swiss WHO headquarters. He has come to do his 'charity', to win some sort of altruistic lottery they ran in his home city. He will go home to acclaim and promotion, wiping the dust of the dark continent from his shoes. Never again to work without making a profit.

Through the bars created by her lashes, she watches him move, taking care to maintain her breathing and stillness. She observes him selfishly making himself coffee here in the Lab so he will not have to share or make others a drink. He does not want others to consider him a servant. At first, she thought this was just a personal quirk, but now she sees his actions for what they are. The petty actions of an entitled man. A man who has assumed his superiority from birth. Never would he question his right to anything that he considers should be his. In three days, he has attempted to ensure they know how lucky they are to have a man of his quality come to rescue them. He oozes arrogance rather than sweat. As she looks down, she sees the leaflet he only half-heartedly tries to conceal. He assumes none of the personnel at the field hospital will understand the complex theories it expounds. All of them, of course, can. She herself holds two doctorates, in

Medicine and Epidemiology. Miriam and Chloe are using their summer break to work on their dissertations, with her as their supervisor. They concealed who they were on his first day, the three conspiring in the joke, telling him the Doctor was in the field. Yet it was they who are taken aback by the way he assumes immediate control.

He places a beaker ready to boil water for his coffee. As he waits for the infusion, he arranges his immunisation area. The tiny vials contain the Salk drops that will prevent the disaster that is polio. In his own country, if you can afford immunisation, this disease only exists in those too poor or ignorant to take care of themselves. Inferior beings in his Darwinian survival-of-the-fittest beliefs. He knows some people are adaptable, but the *superior* adapt better and faster. He knows he has to boost his profile. A citation of his generous pro bono work in the third world will get him into better practice partnerships. Then he arrived here to discover the ignorant and inferior in abundance. He must work in appalling conditions, with only three female assistants. Giggling girls who need direction and make it impossible for him to transfer to a decent hospital. Not this clinic at the arse end of the world. He cannot move on until he gets the Doctor here to sign him off to return to the city.

It was Miriam who brought the deaths to her attention. She had been going out to do the follow-up interviews with the families who had been recently immunised, all part of her dissertation research. One family suffering tragic death was not unknown, and the resources were not available as yet to chase down these cases. Miriam's study was in hope of raising some funding for in-depth research.

Miriam brought the evidence to her of the four families' demise. How they had scoured the records and interviewed the contacts of the families. The only common contact was him. It was hard to believe at first. Entire villages were immunised in a day. As a field unit, they are due to move to a new location next week, but there has been nothing like this mortality in the six months she has been here.

So she watched him, became more vigilant. All three women opted to play along with his perceived opinion of them. His self-confidence allowed him to be almost blatant. His assumption they did not understand his mother tongue meant he commented on the people and the women openly. She used her Dictaphone to record his misogyny and various prejudices.

His rage exploded yesterday when the little ones spied on him in the shower. They told Miriam later it was only to see if he was painted. And in places he was. Miriam told the children it was called a sunwheel.

Last night they had discovered three more families dying. It was time. Action had to be taken

She hears his breathing alter, the beaker break, a soft thud then a crack. They will have to clean up the mess later when they return from work. They will find the body after the clinic. Complain loudly that he had not been with them to help.

She raises her head from her crossed arms. Raises her arms above her head, stretching her back and neck as she sits upright in her chair. She remembers the episode of CSI that showed that some eye drops could be fatal when imbibed. She coated the bottom of his coffee cup with three of the powerful drops so the liquid evaporated overnight, for the crystals to be enlivened again by strong coffee. Out here a death, even of an overseas volunteer, will be taken as unfortunate. Some charity workers do not adapt to the conditions required of them in third world climates or even some inner cities. She will write her condolences to the family after she has done her rounds. She will call her father, and he will ensure her the right things are done. Yes, she was his little shadow. She had recovered from this insidious disease. The shadow that was her brother had not. She will not see her father's work demeaned. Will not see her brother's life negated by a rich, selfish man.

She pushes up on the arms of the chair and kicks out to lock her leg splint. Then she stands as if it is time to start rounds. Preventable polio paralysed the lower joints of her right leg, and she will do what she can to stop it from injuring and killing more innocent people. Whatever is needed.

* * *

* * *

G.L. Waring began her working life as a costumier, which still comes in handy for Dungeons and Dragons. She took a Bachelor of Science degree in Nursing, which she practiced for many years. Whilst raising two daughters, she achieved a Masters degree in Anatomy and a PhD in Philosophy, and finished her career as a lecturer. With a longstanding interest in medieval weaponry, she now makes herself useful to writers of historical mysteries.

# GRIDLOCK - KAREN'S STORY
## A POEM

### JIM TAYLOR

Back in 2035 we set off from Manchester
to Ilfracombe, about two hundred and fifty
    miles Dad said when I asked, how far.
Down the M6, before Crewe,
the lane of crawling cars slowed, stuttered
    until eventually, we stopped.
We sat for a long time, got out, walked
    down the line, talked to other cars,
    then wandered into fields at the road-
    side, or woodlands not far away.
Food was brought by motorcyclists
    weaving between the cars.
On the third day we moved, only half a
    mile. It was April, cool and showery.
Helicopters came over dropping more
    food, it was Easter.
There was plenty of chocolate later,
    donated by overstocked supermarkets.
    We slept in the car.

On the eighth day the helicopter came over
    again, calling to us offering to airlift us
    out, but we didn't want to leave the
    car, it was new and all our tackle was
    in it, so we stayed.
Three months later we reached Solihull.
The weather was better and two lanes
    over, two cars down, a baby was born
    in a Citroen.
I liked the M5, the baby was called Alison.
    They used to push her in the pram,
Up and down the hard shoulder in
    October.
We still wanted to reach Ilfracombe, but
    near Bristol there was a big row.
My dad left in a Peugeot with a woman,
    who was planning to go back to
    Birmingham.
We carried on with Mum and Dave, an AA
    man two cars behind, Mum always did
    like uniforms. We listened to the radio.
It was exciting sometimes, knowing we
    were making history.
Near Exeter I met Danny. I was seventeen,
And he'd just had his nineteenth birthday.
We walked down the line trying to swap a
    tin opener for a torch.
He had long dark hair and wide eyes.
There was an Astra not far off, abandoned.
    We'd heard them talking, with the
    windows down.
We knew they were giving up.

You're not so adaptable when you're
    getting on, using the little stoves,
    looking for insulation for the winter.
It's been over twelve months.
With Dave I think we'll get there,
People round about like him a lot. He's
    very useful, being in the AA
he's teaching my Danny bits now and
    then.
We're only forty miles away now.
I'd like the baby to be born in Ilfracombe.

\* \* \*

*Copyright © Jim Taylor*

\* \* \*

# ACKNOWLEDGMENTS

All proceeds from this book go towards the eradication of polio. A charity anthology is a work of compassion and commitment. There are many people to thank.

Our deep gratitude to the authors, who improbably made time in their demanding schedules to contribute stories. Also to Ann Bloxwich who originally suggested the idea for this book.

David Penny was our editor and is my friend and mentor. This book wouldn't exist without him.

John Laurence provided help and support when words failed me.

We owe our cover design to Emma Taylor, with thanks to her daughter Ava for the handprint! John Leggott College, Scunthorpe, provided design help and resources.

My thanks to the Rotary Club of Scunthorpe, for continuing support throughout the long journey to the book's publication. Fellow Rotarians from other districts also stepped in when help was needed.

We are grateful to the North Lincolnshire Children's Literacy Trust and an anonymous donor for funding.

My comrades The Old Peculiars cajoled their friends and colleagues in the crime and thriller world into contributing stories. Thank you for many years of love and support.

Finally, the world owes a debt to the field workers who are on the front lines every day, collaborating with Rotary International to end polio now.

Lorraine Stevens

Publisher

July 2023

# WHY PURPLE FOR POLIO?

We have used a purple wash on the cover of this story collection because the colour is connected with the fight to end polio.

To ensure a vaccine isn't administered to a child more than once, immunisation workers mark each child's little finger with indelible ink after they receive the vaccine. Indelible or phosphoric ink is made using silver nitrate, which lends the ink a violet-blue colour that fades to purple-brown on the skin. In some countries, a dye derived from gentian violet obtains the same effect.

Whilst there's no account of who chose a purple crocus to represent the promise made by Rotary International and its partners to eradicate polio, it has become an enduring symbol.

World Polio Day is towards the end of October, the bulb-planting season in the Northern hemisphere. The crocuses flower in February, coinciding with World Polio Week.

In association with Rotary International, millions of crocus corms are planted every year, often coordinated with local schools and children's groups. When the flowers emerge in the spring, they provide a reminder that more work is to be done, and are a symbol of hope.

Made in the USA
Coppell, TX
09 October 2023

22617230R00143